SEEING DOUBLE

KAREN RUNGE

GREY MATTER

P R E S S

CHICAGO

SEEING DOUBLE
ISBN-13: 978-1-940658-79-7
ISBN-10: 1-940658-79-9
Grey Matter Press First Trade Paperback Edition - July 2017

Copyright © 2017 Karen Runge
Design Copyright © 2017 Grey Matter Press
Cover Design Copyright © 2017 Dean Samed

GREY MATTER
P R E S S

CHICAGO

Grey Matter Press
greymatterpress.com

Grey Matter Press on Facebook
facebook.com/greymatterpress.com

DEDICATION

For Jürgen.
My brother, my best friend.

PROLOGUE

I want your hands on me. Hard fists, crushing fingers. I want your touch to leave bruises I can look at later, marks I'll see and know that this happened. Really happened. Evidence that you touched me, exactly in these places; circles on my skin that will fade unless I push them, prod them, squeeze them back from yellow to black.

A torture to take pride in.

I want you to grab my hair in fistfuls and cover my mouth with yours, so I can smell you, taste you. The fury in you, the bite. Your stubble scraping my skin, your scent in my nose. I want your kiss to devour me. I want you to clip my tongue with your teeth, my flesh that you'll swallow. Blood in saliva, mixed between us.

This chemistry of heaven that we make in hell.

I want you to hurt me like you love me like you hate me. I want you to make me bleed. I want you to fuck me in the ass with a knife up my cunt—double-edged, cold—adding slits to my slits and putting holes in my holes. Sweetness and blood for you to feel, to taste. And even if you spit it out, the taste of me will remain.

I'm not trying to titillate you, you bastard. Looking at me, smug-serious, your ego screaming in your ears. So loud I almost hear it. Congratulating yourself on how weak you think this makes me. That I want this. That I've asked for this. To love and hate and fuck and ruin.

I want you to destroy me because this is how I destroy you. How I will make sure I remember you. How you will never be able to forget me.

I want you to do this, you sick fuck. This man I love.

I want you. I want you to. I do.

SPRING

ONE

They were married in Wales, in a grey stone church with a view out onto a lake. It was an early spring, too warm for the time of year. The smell of the water was somehow salty, somehow spoiled, vile and thick. Like fish guts and rotting waterweeds. But it came light and crisp too, cooling the air, and Ada turned her face into it when the wind blew her way.

She left her hair loose down her shoulders, curling it as an afterthought, spirals that softened quickly in the heat and lay in soft knots and tangles. She did not wear a veil. Her lipstick was a scarlet so rich it was almost blue — a deep red, a whore red, shrieking against the pale pink and baby blue flowers Daniel's mother had picked out for her bouquet.

Women wear pink lipstick to make men think of their labia, she thought as she coloured her mouth, that final touch before they left for the church. *Women who wear red want them to think of blood.* She capped the tube. She smiled at her reflection.

Ada would have worn a red dress too if Daniel's mother hadn't interfered, blanching at her daughter-in-law's tastes.

"Why should I wear white?" Ada asked. "It's not my colour."

"It isn't a *colour*. It's symbolic of purity," Daniel's mother said.

"But I'm not pure. I'm not a virgin. I'm not even a Christian. Why should I care?"

Like a rebellious teenager she prodded like this, provoked like this. Grinning maleficence into her future mother-in-law's shocked face.

It was a small ceremony. *Intimate.* The word people use to describe weddings that are poorly attended. Immediate family, a handful of friends, a minister. A bare clutch of the unwelcome, welcomed for reasons of social politics. This last included Daniel's aunt, two of his old university friends, and Ada's stepmother, Gabriella.

"It's such a shame for a young bride to be so alone on her wedding day." Gabriella said loudly as they gathered outside the church.

"I wouldn't have wanted all those people staring at me anyway," Ada said, her gaze fixed over the woman's shoulder. And some thought this was sour grapes, but the groom knew better. He stood with his back to them, pretending to talk to his mother. Only Ada knew from his rigid stance, the way his head was cocked slightly to the side, that he was listening to her instead.

"It was just too short notice," Ada's father said, his hand heavy on hers. His eyes were still bloodshot from jetlag. His suit was creased. "You understand."

I do, but you don't, she thought with such venom she might have said it out loud if Daniel hadn't looked over at her just then, turning, his mother struck dumb mid-sentence. He smirked at Ada with blood in his glare. He winked.

This is a charade, that glare said. *This is a game,* that wink said. *We do this and then it's over. We do this and then we're gone.*

This was the deal that had been made.

Ada was married in a town she'd never before visited, in a country not her own. She was married before strangers.

She saved most of her smiles for the groom, and she smiled only once at her father in that final moment as he released her at the altar. A gentle squeeze of her elbow, him for her. A flash of her teeth, her to him. She turned her shoulder. She looked Daniel in the eye. And a secret passed between them.

The air in the church smelled like crushed flowers, clammy skin, expensive perfume. The pews held the scents of wood and dust and history. And up at the altar, there was something else. Something like cold water steaming on warm stones, dusty and earthy, electrified. Holy water sizzling on cursed effigies. Or maybe it was just the smell of the lake drifting in through cracks in the windows and doors. This last she breathed in, deep.

She and Daniel stood very straight with the minister between them, *presiding*. Priest, president and master of the ceremony, the only one present with the power to bind. They didn't look at him. Instead they faced each other with their shoulders squared, their heads tilted back. As though they were challenging each other. Opponents waiting for the count before they began their duel. But they each had the hint of a smile softening the hard edges of their mouths. Ada's fingernails, painted red to match her lips, dug into the fragile stems she held in her hands. A few pink petals drifted to the stone floor. Her cheeks flared, but she said, "I do." And Daniel said, "I do."

And it was done.

* * *

"I used to call my mother Fishy when I was a kid," Daniel told Ada that night. "Because of that glassy look she gets in her eyes when she's shocked by something. Her mouth opening and closing like that. She looks just like a dumb fucking fish. Flapping around, struggling to breathe. It's her signature expression when she thinks you're being 'out of order.'"

Ada thought of broken machines.

She traced the pattern of the bedspread with a freshly manicured finger—that violent shade of red not yet chipped. "She's given you that look a few times too, huh?"

"Oh, you have no idea."

She laughed. "I think I have some."

She lay across the bed, the curves of her shoulder and hip ribboning a loose M against the maroon bed sheets. Maroon for a bridal bed. To save the bride the shame of her blood, maybe. A step in the opposite direction to the older tradition of using white, only white—symbolic, pure—for new husbands to revel in the stains.

I fucked her and she bled.

I fucked her, and I was first.

They lay close against each other, talking. His fingers wrapped in the tangles and knots of her hair, her hand flexing around his penis so that its limp weight thickened into a greasy curve. Like a fattening slug, semi-turgid, softening back to frail human flesh. The texture reminded Ada, uneasily, of Gab's new jowls—those soft weights tacked on either side of her stepmother's chin. Beauty slumping, sliding barbs under the woman's tongue. She thought of her father, dazed and well-meaning, his watery eyes liquid like those of a piddling puppy, kicked.

"I'm free of them now," she said. She felt giddy, overwhelmed. Grinning at her fingernails, she didn't catch Daniel's smile.

The inn had left them a bottle of champagne in a bucket of ice and two crystal glasses. Antique, neatly cut, one stem chipped. The couple left the ice to melt and drank on the bed, the fine little glasses twirled in their hands, forgotten on the bedside tables, retrieved. They drank slowly, which was unusual for them. Impotent froth and sour-sweet sips.

For a little while, they slept.

In the early hours of the morning Ada began to bleed, a stain on the sheet beneath her shaped like a crescent moon.

She cursed the timing, showered alone and fashioned a tampon out of toilet paper. Then she took two painkillers and lay back down beside her husband. She kissed his forehead with a soft touch of her lips. His beard had already thickened on his chin, a darkening growth above his upper lip and along the edge of his jaw. He was naked, the sheets tangled around his waist. Free of fabric from the waist up, his bare skin shimmered pale and vulnerable in the fragile dawn light. She stared at him. The sparse chest hair that twirled out between dark pores, the slim shoulders, the arms so slender they might have been a woman's. And his face, slack, his consciousness vanished.

I'll remember him like this, she thought. *Always exactly like this.*

Before they checked out, she rinsed the two crystal glasses, wrapped them in a summer dress and hid them in her suitcase.

And then they left Wales.

* * *

They went to Cambodia for their honeymoon. A corner of Asia still exotic to them, with its jungle heat and battered streets. They hiked into the forests and walked through ancient, abandoned temples that stood in silence, roped with vines, their ornate stone walls trapped beneath roots that cascaded down like long fingers, gripping the rock without quite crushing it. Back in town, they followed a friend's advice and found the restaurant that served pizza laced with marijuana, cunningly disguised on the menu as HAPPY HERB. The taste of it was like dust and green caught in cheap cheese. It roiled in their stomachs and gave them each a thick, throbbing headache that wrapped them in sick lethargy. Back at the hotel, they sat out on the veranda and drank a cheap Chilean chardonnay. They didn't speak. In the evening they joined on their hotel bed and merged with the heat. The two of them alone. Spent.

She bit the tip of his penis, but he didn't let her draw his blood.

When the honeymoon ended they flew back to the charmless block of Asia they had made their home. They painted their landlord's dingy walls a rich shade of burgundy, cursed the shoddy modern furniture he would not remove, unfurled their new rugs and confessed to their friends what they had done.

"You got married when you were away?"

"Yes," Daniel nodded, taking Ada's hand across the table.

"Oh come on," Ada said at the looks of shocked delight in their friends' faces. When she rolled her eyes she looked disconcertingly like a preteen girl, garishly painted. Her lipstick was still too dark. "These days marriage is just something you do to shut the old folks up."

"And to solve visa issues," Daniel said.

She nodded. "Yes, that too."

Melinda was still gaping at them. "But—I mean—*married!* It's funny, you know. I did think of you. Or maybe it was sort of a premonition. About two weeks ago we were coming out of the subway, and I could've sworn I saw you two crossing the street ahead of us. Anthony spotted you, too. We were going to try catch up with you, or call you up, but then I said 'No Anthony, that can't be Daniel and Ada. Daniel and Ada are in England.'"

"Wales."

"Wales. Europe anyway."

"And Cambodia after, for the honeymoon," Ada said.

"Oh it was Cambodia you went to! Tell!"

And so the first sighting went by barely mentioned, almost unnoticed. A flash in the crowd on a busy street. A glimpse of a couple walking away, vanishing in the crush. Their heads down, their steps in time. Sunlight kissing the backs of their necks.

TWO

L isten. You don't know this about me. The way I bat-
tled my own will to get to where I am now. The way
I've had to split myself, alter myself. Not so much a
chameleon changing shades. Not even so much a leopard
changing its spots. More a full-force shape-shift: supernatural, fantastical. At times even horrific. But above all, extreme.

I was fourteen years old the first time. He was seventeen.
He was taller than you, and skinny. He took the same short-
cut home from school. A path through an open lot behind
the sports field, yellow grass and hissing crickets, heat and
open sky. But mostly heat. There was a path through there,
narrow, dusty, patterned with devil thorns. If you crossed
it barefoot it'd make you bleed. I wore school shoes, brown,
with laces. Or maybe it was buckles. No, laces. I hated the
buckled ones. They made me think of Alice in Wonderland,
or very little girls who dreamed of rabbit holes and didn't
know how far they could fall. I wore brown school shoes,
laces, white ankle socks because it was summer. Remember,
I told you. The heat. Sweat on the back of my neck, scabs
on my shins from wounds opened by the grass. Every blade
sharp enough to cut.

He liked to whistle. I'd hear him coming up behind me. And he walked fast because his legs were so long. In the beginning he'd shove past me and carry on, head down. Shirt sleeves rolled up, waist untucked, school tie flapping over his shoulder like a long black tongue. A black tongue with yellow stripes. Diagonal. He went to the same high school as me. I knew by the tie. He was a few years ahead of me. I knew by the stripes.

I never saw him much between classes. Or maybe I did and just didn't think about it. The way we think, process, is so different when we're young like that. The way we compartmentalise. Training for adult denial, maybe. Or maybe we do the same thing now, too. We just won't know until we're older, much older, and get to reflect again on such a large piece of our lives. See it as a whole. The whole is endless, though none of us really look at it like that.

Alice in Wonderland. Alice and her holes.

In the beginning he'd push past me like the path was crowded, like I was in his way and he was angry with me. Annoyed, I should say. He never glanced back, just shoved. For a moment, an instant of maybe half a step, we shared the path. One foot wrapped in long yellow grass, the other crushing thorns. And me caught between. I want to say there's something symbolic there, but that would be trite. I think that would be trite, because this isn't about symbols. This is something much more solid than that.

He had a long face, sucked-in cheeks. High cheekbones and a wide jaw, so the shape of his face was like a Roman numeral, a capital I. The forehead, the jaw, the line of the nose. His cheeks sucked in, skull-like, creating absences in his face, one on each side when you looked him head-on. This too sounds like symbolism. It's not.

He hadn't quite grown a beard. Not yet. But the hairs on his upper lip were long and black and fine. Like paintbrush hairs, disassembled, spread. His lips were full, like his mouth was swollen. Red lips, thick. You knew just by looking they were very soft.

He was repulsive. You don't understand. He was hideous. Skeletal and bony so even his fingers looked sharp. Tapered tips, swollen knuckles. The nails were too long. The colour, yellow. As if they'd been stained with nicotine or had earwax caked beneath.

He gave me a cigarette, once.

Talking to me in a shy voice that seemed to come from the base of his throat, so that his words were half swallowed and sometimes he was difficult to understand. I had to keep saying, "What? Sorry, what?" And I know it made me look shy. Made me look like he made me shy. Nervous. But really I was trying to be nice. Nice because I thought that was the right way to be. Back then.

He talked to me. Walked with me. I couldn't stand to look at his face. Those hard angles, that mouth like a ripped wound, those delicate black hairs fluffed across his upper lip in nauseatingly delicate wisps. He licked his lips too often, chapping them, cracking them. Thick pink tongue sweeping across, scouring the flesh red. Hair and skin. Black and pink. Soft and wet, splitting. And that was especially repulsive. Vile to watch.

I watched.

When he walked with me I felt dizzy, sick. I kept my hands clenched on the straps of my backpack. I looked at my feet, his feet. I turned my head so that I saw only my feet and imagined I was walking alone.

Once I looked at the growth on his upper lip and thought of licking it flat. My tongue on those hairs, tasting that soft swell. And I was so nauseated I blushed, crossed my arms over my chest, shook my head. I think I even gasped, hissed air back in between my teeth. I do that even now sometimes. Gasp for no reason. Clench myself in. When memories, flashes, images, ricochet through my head. You've heard me do it, I think.

I saw myself licking the skin above his swollen red lip. I wouldn't look at him again after that. Not for a while. A day, a week. I don't know. I don't know what he thought. I know what he thought. What he must've thought. I think.

He walked with me. He talked with me. He gave me a cigarette. I tried to be nice. His skin was rubbery, turgid. He didn't brush his teeth.

"You don't like me," he said, grinning at me like he didn't believe it. Like he was saying what he thought was an opposite to get at what he thought was a truth.

Which was not.

"Yes I do," I said.

But I did not.

"Prove it," he said. Walking off the path, his back to me, and the sun behind me so my shadow tapered out ahead, long and loose and liquid, touching him where he stood. Like I was reaching for him.

But I was not.

"Come on," he said, turning to face me. "Prove it." Loosening his tie. A noose. Opening his shirt. A void.

I looked away. I looked again. He was so thin his ribs rolled up against his skin. He had three nipples. A mutant mole. He dropped his shirt into the long grass. It hung there like an abandoned flag, trembling in the wind that twitched the tips of the grass where it touched. A white flag. A call for surrender, thrown down in the field. He took off his pants. His hips were as bony as the rest of him, like blades jutting out, sliding under his skin when he moved.

"Now you," he said. Grinning at me like I was such a sure thing. Yellow teeth, scarecrow fingers. I imagined his taste: mouldy, sour. I imagined that touch: scratching, sharp. I felt chill against the heat, with sweat sliding down my back, slipping down the cleft between my new A-cup breasts. My skin stippled with goose bumps. I didn't move. Instead I stood with my shadow touching him, my shoes crushing thorns.

Until he crossed back to the path toward me, kicking through the grass. Until he came for me.

He was taller than me. I told you that. So much taller. That's why I bit my tongue when I hit the ground, slicing into it with my teeth. Crescent moon wound. A trickle of blood got caught in my throat. The taste of violence I've never spat out.

What are you doing? I asked myself. Fists clenched. Kicking my legs. *What am I doing?* Struggling to breathe.

I wanted the earth to open up beneath me, to create a hole I could fall into. But there was no hole. Not underneath. Only within. I fell down it anyway—fell laughing or crying, even now I'm not sure. Blood and broken grass and thorns in my back.

Alice and her holes.

You know something about falling. I saw in you the echo of a scream, caught. A blood-tone sound, voiceless. Only those who've swallowed it themselves can recognise it in others. Almost from the moment I first saw you, I heard it— that cry stuck in your throat. Our paths were different, but we came to this place together, I think. We fell together, I think.

Where's Daniel? I want to try and say this to Daniel. He might hear me now, if you could bring him here. If you'd let him come. Please let him. Where's Daniel?

It's cold in here.

THREE

Their apartment block was in the heart of the city, a calm zone of historical sections and residential areas surrounded by a circling highway. The zone itself tranquil, the world beyond it frenzied. The narrow roads within traversed irregular blocks of battered stone walls and whitewashed store fronts like the thin, broken veins of an old heart. This heart beat slowly, steadily. The heart of a beast in hibernation, or a monk in a trance. This was what it felt like, living in that place. Like being lost in unreality, like growling in your sleep.

The city as a whole was vast and ugly, its long history razed to a whisper as most of the older buildings were torn down, replaced with cheap mock-ups or garish modern structures. Even in the calm centre, it was a city insane with contradictions. Rickshaws and Lamborghinis. Neon lights and dusty lanterns. Prada shoes and broken feet. Its beauty, when revealed, seemed sometimes almost accidental. Battered furniture abandoned in an alley, plush with morning dew. A splintered wooden door hanging off its hinges, its rich patina struck stark with age. A songbird in an ornate cage, hung in the eaves. Swinging. Singing.

Daniel and Ada's building was one of several in a gated compound, all built in the 70s, all with broken steps and tricky plumbing and sound-activated lights flashing on and off in the stairwells. Their apartment was one of many in the area that had been "renewed." Retiled, repainted, sinks replaced and cabinets installed. The gleaming interior a surprise to see against the building's peeling paint and rain-stained face.

Their neighbourhood was composed of one-way streets locked in a cryptic grid only locals or long-time residents could comfortably navigate. Here the buildings were low, old, the eaves scalloped, the walls painted grey to disguise the dust. Fruit and vegetable shops crammed with produce did their commerce through open windows and narrow doorways. There were print shops, convenience stores, tearooms and noodle stands. In the narrow, zigzagging alleys that shot free of the one-way streets there were sometimes wardrobe-sized art exhibitions where lanky local men and svelte local girls smoked cigarettes and sipped table wine out of cheap glasses. This too was sometimes ugly, sometimes beautiful. But mostly it was beautiful.

Locals and foreign residents rode scooters and bicycles to the nearby subway station, where locks and prayers kept their property, mostly, safe from the scruffy youths with tricky fingers who haunted the bicycle racks. Most of the residents worked in the new business districts that lay staggered around the city, far from the calm heart's reach. They rode the trains into those outer places, into sections dense with sleek high-rises and wide streets where offices, duties and alter egos waited to claim them. There were fewer lanterns there and more neon. And always the rush and roar coming in from the streets outside the glass-walled offices. Traffic, sirens, raised voices and thousands and thousands of swift-stepping feet. This was the cacophony Ada hated most, worse every day, living within a gradually shrinking circumference, fighting to shut the world beyond it out. And so one day she went to the subway station and forgot she no longer carried her metro card.

Because a month after the wedding she'd quit her job, of course.

"I don't need to work," she said. "You're making more than enough for the two of us." And when Daniel's eyes changed, she grinned.

"You want to be a…a *housewife*?"

She put a hand on his arm. A caress that dared to tighten. "I can think of worse things I could be. To you."

"You're brutal," he said. But he laughed.

Her life slowed. Cleaning and cooking and kissing him goodbye, kissing him hello. The air in their apartment thick with her constant presence; scented soap and thin sweat, the incense she burned almost obsessively clinging to the curtains, the upholstery, her clothes. There were many women like her in their neighbourhood, foreign and local alike. *Housewives.* Fat thickening beneath their filmy dresses, hair clipped back in slovenly chic with tortoiseshell barrettes. Many of them went out pushing prams, holding tiny hands, rubbing swollen bellies with protective glee. They bought their fruit and vegetables from the same hole-in-the-wall store Ada did, their bread and meat from the same German bakery/butchery Ada did, sashayed down the same broken streets as her. Fat feet in ballet flats, frowning at Ada's red leather jacket, her tousled hair, her blood-shock lipstick.

No, I am not you, she thought, glaring back at them. *I am not like you. Not like you. I am. Not.*

But she did, now, have a ring to flash around. Sometimes when she felt these women's eyes on her, she rubbed her chin with her left hand — deliberately, conspicuously, like it made any difference. Like she didn't feel small and petty for doing it. For even feeling the need.

It was only late at night as she lay sleepless beside her husband that her sense of smug satisfaction became palpable unease.

Housewife.

What was that? What did it mean? Or, what did it mean for her? She lay staring up at the ceiling, listening to the footfalls that echoed through the building's thin walls as she pulled the word apart—finding anagrams that frightened her, telling herself they were not codes, *not* codes. That they were just coincidences, accidents of the English language, and not to be taken too seriously.

House Wife Wise How
Fuse She He
Who? Foes
Whose? His
He we of I us
Hew use of I

And on until her head ached and her jaw throbbed from clenching her teeth, and she woke with migraines so bad she came back to herself wondering if she'd gone blind in the night. Lying beside him with her hands over her eyes.

FOUR

People talk about trauma like it's an excuse. Is it? I don't know.

This thing Daniel and I did, those things we did before you, with you, without you. To you. Those things you did to us. I sometimes think it comes from somewhere else. There are hints of it embedded deeper in the fabric of our lives, in the things that came before. Look for yours. I've looked for mine.

Before that day in the field. Long before, when I was still a child. Before my body began its natural shape-shift and turned me into something else. Once a year we stayed at my uncle's farm, so he and my father could go trout fishing. They did this every year, and I'm told I always went with. But I don't remember the other times. The times before this. Or after. Memories like dreams, too muted to be real.

But this I know. I remember this.

My uncle was younger than my father. He was hand-some — I knew that even then. Dark hair, dark eyes. Off-centre smile. He was cheeky and gregarious and sometimes a little dangerous. I knew that, too. He liked to sit me on his lap and pinch my knees. He'd jiggle his own knee with me astride it and say we were "riding horsey." It made me laugh. It made my father and uncle laugh, too. My laughter bright and free, my uncle's thick and deep and too loud in my ear until my father said, "Enough now, hand her back to me." Smiling, trying to smile. Picking me up, high in his arms. Holding me against him. Turning away.

Then.

I think I was six. Seven, maybe. They went out early in the morning dressed in waterproof jackets and gum boots. They left carrying rods and cooler boxes and tidy little bags filled with neatly arranged hooks. Beautiful hooks. Fly-fishing hooks. Feathered, threaded. Made to look like brightly coloured water insects — designed as tricks, traps, lures. They were called nymph hooks, my uncle told me the night before. And told me not to touch them, not to play with them. When he left the room I did it anyway. Running my fingertips along the tight-wound threading and bits of bird feathers. Brown, green and brightest electric blue. It seemed obvious to me that no fish would fall for this. Fantastical food too dazzling to be real. Alluring colours dancing along deadly metal arcs. They wouldn't believe the colours, I thought. They wouldn't bite down on those barbs.

Nymphs.

I pressed my finger to the end of a hook, testing its sharpness. Focus-point of pain. I pressed a little harder. The tip popped into the soft cushion of my thumb and called up a drop of blood. I put my finger in my mouth. I tasted it. Sweet metal, bright on my tongue.

Nymph. A word I didn't understand, then. But understood that it was a kind of death trap, presented in dazzling disguise.

My uncle and my father got back in the early afternoon with a cooler box full of fish. Trout. Rainbow trout. Sleek and fat and shining, with pretty colours painted along their sides.

But no blood. I didn't see any blood. My uncle opened the cooler box to show me the catch and all I saw were twitching bodies and wide, translucent eyes.

"They're still moving," I said.

"Don't worry," he smiled, drawing me close to him at the waist. "They're dead."

"Then why are they still moving?"

"They do that even after they're dead."

I stared into the box, sick with wonder. *Dead?* I thought. *Dead things don't move.*

"You want to watch me descale them?" he asked, his fingers tightening, almost hard enough to hurt. "Gut them?"

Off-centre smile.

Descale means peel. Removing the tough outer layer of sharp, shiny little flakes that would slice our tongues and the insides of our cheeks. And gut means eviscerate. Slitting bellies, releasing blood. Pulling the entrails out in their slippery stream of connected knots. Emptying the fish out. Cleaving holes. Leaving them hollow.

"While they're still alive?" I asked.

His fingers tightened on my waist. "They're dead."

Can dead things move? Can live things lie still?

We went to the courtyard, out the kitchen door. He opened the box and took the fish out. And this time they didn't just twitch, they jumped. Sleek silver bodies flashing in the air as they flopped and turned and spun. Fell. Lay still on the rough concrete. Gasped. Then thrashed, then leapt. Again. He grabbed them one at a time, hunched over them, holding them against his knees, scraping a blade along their bodies as they squirmed and jerked in his hands. Gasping mouths. Rainbow scales falling like fairy confetti, catching the light at my feet.

"They're still alive," I said. Said standing very still, my hands over my mouth, my heart skittering, leaping. Just like the fish.

"They're dead."

And he cut them open, throat to tail, their insides slipping out of them in pink ribbons, looped and frilled, organs drooping like bunches of quivering flowers.

They're dead, I told myself. *They're dead.*

But they moved.

"Most girls would cry," my uncle said after, washing off his hands. And I knew I'd impressed him somehow. "You're like a tough little boy trapped in a pretty little body, aren't you?" He ran a still-wet hand through my hair. And he called me that name. He said, "Nymph."

Fish blood and drops of water sparkled on my cheeks. I said it to myself: Dead things move. Said it over and over again, still struggling to believe.

We had those fish for dinner. Roasted in the oven, dressed with olive oil and garlic and a mess of bright green herbs.

I hate trout. It tastes like mud, like river dregs, like waterweeds and soiled tissues. I doused mine in mayonnaise and ate it anyway. Tangy murk soft between my teeth, sliding down my throat.

"Have some more," my uncle said.

And I did. Chewing slowly, carefully. Waiting for the feel of flesh twitching in my mouth. Wanting it, not wanting it. Dreading it, hoping for it.

Dead things moving. Live things lying still.

That night I had nightmares about the fish in my belly. Rainbow scales skittering through my guts in paper-thin shards, sharp as shattered glass. Ripping me open. I felt the fish jumping inside of me, pushing at the walls of my body. Scales and fins and hooks through mouths. A hook in my own mouth, stopping my screams.

When I woke the next morning I was dizzy, damp with sweat. The taste of river water dark in the back of my mouth.

Trauma, this wasn't. I don't think so. Do you?

FIVE

C ome and meet Cassandra," Daniel said. "Ada, this is Cassandra. Cassandra, this is my wife, Ada. She's an artist."

She's an artist.

Not *housewife*. This word he couldn't quite yet use in relation to the woman he'd married.

The girl smiled up at Ada, a pint of beer in her hand. Swallowing. Smiling. "Hey! Daniel's told me so much about you."

Ada tossed her handbag onto the empty seat beside Cassandra. It landed with a *thump* that made the girl jump, then laugh.

Ada smiled. She sat.

"Cass is a freelance graphic designer," Daniel said. "She just finished up a project with us. She's good. We might use her again."

"Really?" The girl jerked up in her seat, almost slopping her beer.

How many has she already had? Ada wondered. She scanned the table for condensation marks. She assessed the state of the coasters. They were cardboard, soaked, the edges peeled. Daniel didn't do that—peel, pick. So this girl was the culprit. Peeling, picking. But why? Nerves? Probably. Getting drunk with a man in a bar can be an exercise in tension.

And then he announces his wife is on the way.

Daniel was drinking his usual predatory afternoon mix of soda water and mint leaves. Leaving out the gin and calling it a *mojito*, which the girl probably didn't think to disbelieve. He would drink later, and too much. But not for a while yet.

Ada ordered a Campari on ice. Her own predatory afternoon drink. Thick and tart and just sweet enough.

"I'm good," the girl said, pre-empting Ada's question and holding up her glass to show it was still half-full. With her free hand she flicked at the edges of a coaster, splitting the layers of paper at the rim.

Yes, you're still good. Peeling. Unpeeled.

The girl had dark hair, thick and tangled. Her eyes, circled with thick black lines, were round, ogling. She reminded Ada of a Tibetan terrier one of her and Daniel's neighbours used to have. Also dark-haired, that hair also thick and tangled, its coat perpetually unkempt. Whenever they came across it in the stairwell it had rolled around at their feet in lunatic self-deprecation, greasy knots of fur falling in its eyes, pink tongue flapping.

And her lipstick is the same shade of pink its tongue was, Ada thought. *Too vivid, too bright against the black. I don't think it matches her labia. It can't.*

She had a sense that Daniel may have wondered about the same thing.

Well, we should find out soon enough.

Unlike the dog, the hair that hung over this girl's eyes was cut. It lay flat across her forehead in a harsh edge. Hiding bad skin, or just giving her something to hide behind. She touched it often, brushing her fingers through it as though it were thick with knots. Another nervous tic. The girl's bra set her cleavage in clear, perfect arcs. Ada could almost make out the faint impressions of the girl's nipples.

Fringe too severe, lipstick too pink, tank top too tight.

The girl grinned at her.

And a sweet little idiot.

"You know," Ada said, "Daniel and I used to come here every Saturday afternoon and drink tequila. It's good here. They serve it in tiny metal shooters, frozen. You know the kind? We should order some."

"Oh, no!" The girl laughed, waving the idea off. She clawed at her forehead, ducking her head. Like a turtle drawing itself in. A shell creature hoping to protect its soft inner parts — the vulnerable hidden parts. Nerves and plush pink organs and tender, blood-rich flesh. "I don't drink tequila, usually."

"Usually?" Ada's smile was still clamped to her mouth. "Why only usually?"

"Oh, you know…same as most people I guess. Sometimes I don't know when to stop. Then I just get really drunk and out of control."

Daniel folded his arms on the table. He leaned in at her, smiling. "You remember any of those stories? Let me guess. One night stands. Or do you get sad and start crying?" He considered her, smirking. "No. I don't think that's you. You're more the kind to start dancing on tables."

"Or stripping on tables," Ada added, and laughed. Her eyes flicked from the girl's cleavage and back to her mouth. Yes, that seemed more like it. For a twenty-something girl with a punk haircut, racy clothes, too much eyeliner. For a young adventurer far from home, still too green to check her actions.

Consequences, Ada thought. *You don't know what those are just yet. But you will.*

Cassandra stared at them, round eyes ogling, mouth agape. She was at risk of sobering up. "I…I can't tell you stories like that," she said. "I might have to work with you again. And I...I've just met you, Ada."

"Come on," Daniel winked. "It happens to us all."

The girl's mouth shifted shape, became a smirk. "To us all? So you strip on tables, do you, Daniel?"

He laughed. "Not quite. But my wife and I love a good, humiliating tequila story. We have a few of our own. Think of it as a bonding thing."

Strong, Ada thought in warning. *Far too strong.*

"Don't push her, Daniel," Ada said, leaning away. "You shouldn't force people to expose themselves like that." Then to the girl, "Sorry. Sometimes it's like Daniel only feels secure around people when he knows some of their secrets."

"No, no...that's okay. To be honest, a beer or two more and I'd probably share without even thinking. You two are fun, I think. For a married couple."

This wasn't meant to sting, but it did. Ada took another swallow. Campari was a short drink and an expensive one. She'd have to switch to beer soon, especially if they were going to be drinking tequila later. Which, she had no doubt, they would be.

We'd better be.

"Thank you," Daniel said. He smiled, but Ada knew that smile — hard-eyed, blood-lit.

"I wasn't much of a drinker before I came here," Cassandra said. "But there really isn't much else to do."

"If you want drugs, Daniel could probably get them for you," Ada said.

The girl gaped again, her mouth a perfect circle hole. "Drugs? In this country? But don't they...don't they *execute* people for that here?"

"Oh, come on," Daniel snorted. "Only for selling. For using they just kick you out. And even then that only happens if you don't know the right people to get you out of it."

"Connections." Cassandra nodded.

"Yes," Daniel said. "And I'm a high-end translator, inter-preter. I couldn't be more connected. Whatever you want, I can get it." His smile loosened. "Just say the word."

The girl glanced around the bar; furtive, tense. "I...I wouldn't want to risk it," she said.

Big Brother paranoia, Ada thought. But she posed a frown for Daniel. "Careful," she said to him, "this is a public place. You never know how much of what you say in English might be understood."

Cassandra looked relieved. She slugged down a mouthful of beer, settling back in her chair. She raised an eyebrow at Ada. "So are you really an artist?"

A twitch ran up Ada's back, jerking her shoulders. A flinch. She nodded at the question—for an instant, almost awkward. "Not really," she said. "I used to teach it, though."

"C'mon." Daniel's hand closed over the nape of her neck. His grip too tight. "You're a brilliant artist."

"I haven't painted anything in a while," Ada said, ignor-ing Daniel's hand. Blocking out the word "brilliant," which seared her in a spotlight of bright acid. Burning. "Lately I find it too frustrating."

"Frustrating?" the girl asked. "What do you mean?"

It was hard for Ada to be clear in moments like this. Try-ing to pick and choose in a split second which parts of herself to express. Which versions of the truth.

"Well, I mean the art that sells here is much more tradi-tional. I don't get excited about mountain views and bowls of fruit. I like to paint things with a bit more of a pulse. Some-thing a little more exciting."

Cassandra leaned in. "You mean like nudes? You look like someone who might paint nudes." She put her hand over her mouth, and giggled. "I think."

Trite little mind, Ada thought, grinning inside.

"Well, no, not necessarily..."

Daniel took his phone out, tapped out a message and rested the phone on his leg. Noticing this, Ada stood and leaned over the table to retrieve her bag. As her proximity to the girl tightened, she made a point of not looking at her. Her hair fell over her shoulder, offering the girl a gift of perfume. "Sorry," she mumbled, and sat back down.

"So you paint...what?"

"Whatever interests me."

"I'm sure it must be brilliant," the girl said, awkwardly enthused. A drop of beer moistened the cusp between her lower lip and the curve of her chin. "I read somewhere that artists who don't shut up about their work are the wannabes, the fakes. And those who don't are the real deal. I think that's true. It must be. I only deal with graphics. Computer graphics, you know? But I think I understand when I hear artists talk. I mean, computer graphics *is* an art, that's true, but in so many ways it really isn't the same. You know?"

Ada nodded, sedate.

Keep her fragile. Keep her trying.

Daniel and Ada's latest little idiot took another large swallow of her beer. She was nervous, drinking like it could help her. Ada studied her again. The messy dark hair, the smooth pale skin. And her chest—plush arcs trapped under thin fabric. Pressing. Nipples tightening.

"I used to draw and paint in school," the girl went on, "but I'm not sure I was any good. I once did a painting of this bowl of cherries, and I used..."

Ada's phone sounded. Daniel's message, delivered. She opened it and read: I WANT TO FUCK HER TITS.

Ada smiled.

SIX

When I was sixteen, I spent the summer holiday at my father's house. He and Gab were still working, leaving me alone during the day in their new home. A new house, the air within thick with the caustic smells of paint and drying plaster. Modern. They used this word when they described it to me over the phone, before I saw the place in the flesh. Their voices crackling down the line, rapid, enthused. Modern. It was. It was white-walled and white-tiled as an asylum might be. As an exhibition space, or a public lavatory. It was open-plan, adding to the vacuous blankness of all that surface area, all that white. Maybe to try and balance this, it had skylights and laminate countertops and blinds that opened and closed on plastic pulls.

The grass outside was green, trim. Not wild, not yellow. No devil thorns to puncture my feet if I walked across it, to rip at my back if I lay down on it. I was glad for that. And in the middle of that lawn there was a hole. Deep, but not endless. Tiled, not vacuous. A circular swimming pool, a perfect O of clear blue water. A safer place to fall into.

It was a summer of water. Before I swam, I bathed. After I swam, I showered. Soap and chlorine and dry skin, my scalp tight, my nose tormented by heat and cold and pool chemicals. Blood sliding from my nostrils in thin trails, dressing my upper lip, feeding its raw salt taste into my mouth. Sweet metal.

Gab kept the freezer stocked with store-bought pizzas wrapped in cellophane. I heated them in the oven and ate them cross-legged in front of the TV, skipping through channels, staring at the screen. Faces, images, voices, sounds. Sick on cheap salami, sometimes I laughed out loud. My voice cracking against those blank white walls.

I was lonely. I was alone. I was afraid to be alone because I was afraid of my own thoughts. I filled my head with TV voices and the sounds of rushing water. I tried not to look into reflective surfaces because there was something different in my eyes. A hollow softness. A harder helplessness. I stepped around my shadow, afraid of how far it might reach.

My father and Gab came home in the evenings. They took me to restaurants, bars. We ate Indian, Vietnamese, Greek. These restaurants all had signature tablecloths — ornate, white, check. They all had special dishes and special ways to eat the food — fingers, forks, chopsticks. This sauce, that sauce. In this order, for that mouthful. That bite. The tables were all square, evenly spaced, lit by flames. Candles, lamps. Things that glow, that slowly burn.

"Are you getting lots of rest?" Gab asked. "Are you having a good time?"

Because she was still trying to win me over, back then.

"I'm sorry we can't be with you more, sweetheart," my father said.

Sorry? I was never sure. Sometimes in these restaurants a look would pass between him and Gab. Commiseration, I think.

It's okay. It will be over soon. It's okay. We'll be alone again soon.

These unspoken words I sometimes heard.

At some of the bars, Gab ordered soda water for me and dumped half her wine into my glass when no one was looking. At other bars, places where the lights were a little dimmer and the tables a lot stickier, she ordered me rum and Coke or vodka and orange juice. Sweet things with teeth. And the bartenders would shake their heads and mix the drinks, grinning and sometimes winking at me as they slid them across the bar.

I see you.

Whenever I got up the room would spin. On my way to the restroom, I'd push through the crush of people and every touch felt like a blow. Too much, too many—hands and shoulders and hips. Ramming me. I'd slam the stall door shut behind me and breathe like I couldn't breathe. Clawing at the lock, my eyes burning. Biting my fingers. Blood on my tongue.

If we stayed late enough, after a while my father and Gab would forget I was there. Pretend to forget. They'd turn toward each other, turn away from me. From across the room it looked like I was sitting alone. Drinking alone. I got up. I wandered. Not wanting to speak, but wanting to be near the pulse of these strangers. Middle-aged men with broad shoulders, beer bellies. Divorced women in too-tight clothes and teased up hair. Raucous, laughing. Far from me.

But they noticed me. Too young, too nervous, sipping my drinks down, chewing the straws. My hair twisted over my shoulder. Gab's lipstick, desperately offered, searing my lips.

"Hey, girl."

"Can I get you another?"

"Hey girl, you here alone?"

I slid on and off the chairs these men offered, stumbled to and away from the bar where they put their arms around me, leaned close to me. Their bleary eyes locked onto me, alcohol loosening their smiles into smirks.

"You're really fucking sexy."

I remember the man who said that to me. Threw it out there like it was a hard admission. Then laughed, like it was funny.

And I asked, "Am I?"

"Yes, you are," he said. "I like you." Then, "Do you like me?"

"Yes," I said. Did I? Didn't I? I didn't know how to tell. Remembering school shoes and devil thorns. Tasting blood in my mouth, blood on my tongue. A phantom wound, burning.

"How old are you?" he asked. "No, don't tell me. However old you are, you're trouble."

Trouble. I smiled at him for that.

I drank the drinks he bought me. He wrapped his arms around my hips and pulled me back against him. A circle around me. Another kind of hole. He pulled me closer. Pressed. And there was a roaring in my ears—a rush that made me close my eyes and lean back into him, resting. Bliss. My head rolling back on his shoulder as his hand slipped under my shirt. Tentative, cautious fingertips trembling against my skin.

When it was time to go, my father called me away. Himself bleary-eyed, his own smile a smirk. Only aimed at Gab, and not at me. He wrapped his arm around my shoulders, pulling me away.

"Who was that man?" he asked.

We were walking out the bar. We were walking through the doors. I was not looking back.

"No one," I said. Because, of course, he was nobody to me.

"You must be careful around men," Gab said, her tone mother-wise, her voice too loud, her words slurred.

"No," I said. "Not me. I'm the trouble, not them."

Trouble.

And my father laughed. And Gab laughed. But neither of them understood.

SEVEN

S unday morning. The morning after. Ada woke in disarray, sunlight striking the windows, smudging shadows
through the dark curtains. She was on the couch, a sheet
wrapped around her. It was caught around her body in knots
and snarls that had tightened as she turned in the night, con-
stricting her ribcage so that she woke from a dream in which
someone was crushing her — arms clamped around her, thick
and soft. God-like in their totality. She woke gasping, a thick
pounding in her head and heat searing between her legs. She
looked to her left and saw the girl slumped beside her. Dark
hair tousled, wild, black-circle eyeliner smudged across her
cheeks. Like she'd been crying. But she hadn't been — had
she? Ada stared, waiting for her to twitch, to snore, something. Anything. The girl was deep in sleep. Drugged sleep.
Lost sleep. That sleep so much like death.

Dead things move, Ada thought. *Live things lie still. We gave
her too much.*

Ada studied the girl. There was a sheen of sweat on her
forehead, a thin line of blood, rust-brown, dried at the edge
of her mouth. But otherwise she seemed all right. A quilt had

been thrown over her, and when Ada drew it back she saw the girl was naked too, legs apart, a bottle resting between her thighs. The residue left on its neck had dried to a fine powder white. *No blood.* The girl's chest rose and fell in shallow breaths. *No blood and not dead.*

She felt strangely happy.

Ada bunched the sheet around herself and limped to the bathroom. She urinated in sharp, acidic bursts that made her hiss through her teeth. She hunched over the sink and brushed her teeth until the froth turned pink. She made her way into the bedroom. Throbbing, stinging.

Daniel lay naked on top of the sheets, his body thin and pale and shadowed.

He's beautiful when he sleeps, she remembered. *His teeth are to the wall.* Who had taught her that expression? The Russian girl, of course. Her and Daniel's second escapade, failed. They'd been lucky to find her, they'd thought, until they got her home and she asked for money. And instead of being angry, the girl was terrified. Or was it that, instead of being terrified, she'd been angry? Ada couldn't really remember anymore.

Every day a clean slate. Close the mind and time draws a veil.

She slid onto the bed, over Daniel's body. Her breasts pressed against his back, her hipbones digging into the soft mounds of his buttocks. He groaned, half waking. She helped him find her hand.

"We're alone?" he mumbled into the pillow.

"No," she said, kissing the soft, scarred skin between his shoulder blades. "She's still out."

"How out?"

"Very out."

"S'time?"

"Still early."

"Good," he groaned, squeezing her fingers. "Good, good."

"But the sun's up."

He yawned into his pillow. "Take care of it, babe," he drawled. And closed his eyes again.

Ada lifted herself up onto her elbows, staring down at the nape of his neck. She blinked her vision clear. She tried to swallow, but her mouth was too dry.

"Daniel," she said, bending closer to his ear.

"Hmmm?"

"You're leaving me with her?"

"What?"

"Please wake up."

He shifted under her, rousing himself. "She's not so heavy," he said. "You'll be all right."

It wasn't the first time Ada wished she wasn't alone.

EIGHT

My first, maybe my real first, I was eighteen. He was nineteen. He was exactly two hundred days older than me. We worked that out. We turned it into a game. Like when he thought I didn't understand something the same way he did, he'd say, "Add two hundred." Like when I thought he was treating me like I was dumb, I'd say, "Add two hundred." And we laughed. This game we played with our impressions of what it meant to be mature.

He said he loved me. I didn't know what to say. I was too aware of the contradictions in me, the ruptures in my personality. Shape-shift separations, divides. Already, I knew they were there. For example, there was that question I always asked in answer: which parts of me do you love?

For example, there was that question I never dared ask: which parts of me can't you love?

And I never said it back: I love you.

I tried to see myself through his eyes. Knowing that the image we each had of me didn't quite match. Like looking at a painting on a wall, then seeing its reflection in a mirror. The same thing, different. The same thing, backwards.

And when you look again at the original, you realise you're choosing what to see.

I was like that. He didn't see me like that. I was like that, to me.

I wanted him close to me — I wanted him far from me. He knew my history, he knew my thoughts. He knew things about me he shouldn't have known. I'd told him things. I'd told too much.

He'd put his fingers in my mouth and sometimes I sucked them, sometimes wanted to bite. Imagined it clearly: the crunch, the blood. The expression in his face of pain and surprise. Shades of horror, shifting in his eyes. His image of me, reversed. Closer to the truth. I fantasised about that; I tormented myself with the fantasy. Wrapped my arms around his neck instead, crossed my legs behind his back. Consumed him with my body. When he collapsed against me, sweat and skin and desperate breath, I never felt so strong. Protective. Resentful. Holding him, then pushing him away.

"Get off of me, you're too heavy."

"Get away from me, I can't breathe."

He still lived with his mother. His bedroom was next to hers, at the top of the stairs. A wall between them. Us. She wore nude makeup like she was still seventeen. Like she was still pretty. When I first saw her she was dressed in jeans, too blue, too tight on the hips and too loose around her legs. A blouse, tucked. Pale paisley print, I think. And then there was me on her doorstep. She stared. Her expression: braced. Then stupefied. Then horrified. Her eyes widening, her lip curling like she'd just been slapped. Like she wanted to slap.

Me, in my sleek black jeans. My low-cut tee. My violent red mouth. Asking, "Is James home?"

And she stared.

When I'd come round before and she wasn't there, I'd wondered about this woman. I'd walked every room in her house: invader, inspector. Seeing things she wouldn't want me to see. Touching things she wouldn't want me to touch. Tampons hidden beneath a collection of handkerchiefs, stuffed in a small woven grass basket by her bed. Pictures of herself on her wedding day, her left shoulder trimmed too close to the frame. Evidence of her former husband, and how he'd been clipped free. She'd decorated her house with the banal taste of a woman who imitates what she finds in magazines. Beige and chic and IKEA made.

That day I asked, "Is James home?"

And I read in her eyes what she wanted to say.

Get away! I think.

Keep your cunt away from my son!

These voiceless things I used to hear. Vicious. Hilarious. And always, far too loud.

It's common for mothers to be horrified at the fact that their sons, even their precious baby boys, are objects and victims of lust. Mothers are supposed to be prepared for this. Still, it comes as a shock.

Not my son, I think they think. Even if he's nineteen.

And so they hate the girls — or boys — who prove them wrong.

And that was me. The one who proved her wrong.

"Is James home?"

My eyebrow raised. My smile a smirk. Almost. Standing on her doorstep, looking past her shoulder. My heart thick in my chest, thundering. Not staring back, though she stared at me. And poison passed between us.

Every time after that he'd rush downstairs when I rang the doorbell. Knowing maybe that she might turn me away. Just might. But mother is one thing, and lover is something else. Each can get away with murder. But not the murder of the other.

Eventually I'd smile at her. Say hello to her. In wounded moments say to him, "Your mother hates me."

And he'd say, "I don't care what she thinks."

Not refuting, not exactly comforting. Still.

I'd take revenge on her by being loud in bed. A trick I'd learned from Gab, knowing it left his mother helpless, tormented. If she listened, I don't know. If she turned the TV volume up, I don't know. Either is possible. Maybe she turned the TV off altogether and masturbated downstairs on her little beige couch, wrenching agony out of herself to the sounds of his headboard banging, the sounds of my exaggerated shrieks. Unzipping her skirt and slipping her fingers down her wide white cotton panties. Leaking stifled dreams.

Once we had sex just as I started menstruating. I left a pool of blood that soaked straight through to the mattress.

"Oh no," he said, horrified, peeling back the sheets. "Oh no!"

I didn't curse the timing. The stain was something she'd have to deal with. Something she couldn't deny.

I was petty like that.

I sucked his fingers, and I wanted to bite.

But I've already told you that.

I hated her, maybe. I loved him, maybe. We lay naked on his bed and smoked cigarettes. The sex was clumsy, rough, sometimes absurd. A boy raised on pornography. He'd only had one other girl before me. He always felt guilty afterward. Like he'd just done something bad to me. That never made sense. This ridiculous, reflexive guilt. A denial of my own senses. Or a misunderstanding of them, at least.

Was that why I did it?

That day, she opened the door to me. I smiled and I didn't smirk. I pushed past her when he came down the stairs. We went to his bedroom. I took off my clothes.

"I'm tired," he said.

"Fuck you," I said. Or maybe I said, "Fuck me."

He didn't want to look at me. His eyes shifting around me like I was a mirage he couldn't see clear.

"I just had a fight with my mother," he said.

As though I wanted to hear anything about his mother, in this place that was his, in the space that we shared.

He said, "No," but he was nineteen, and few things can outweigh this promise: my body is yours.

This promise I made.

I lay on his bed, on my side. Bare and eighteen with my hair falling over my shoulder. Sliding my hand between my legs.

"Please don't do that," he said. "I don't know if I can." Standing by his window, hesitant. Fully-clothed against me.

"Yes you can," I said.

He wanted me to hug him, talk to him. Be a friend to him. Did I want to do that, be that? I wasn't sure. Looking at him, and the hurt in his eyes. Shutting it out.

"Come on," I said.

And he came to me easily enough. His penis still flaccid. A vulnerable curl, a boneless finger, soft and sensitive in baby pink. Saying, "Not now. I can't and I don't want to."

But standing where I kneeled.

I didn't bite. I wanted to. I know it crossed my mind. How easy it would be to bring my teeth together in that moment. Feel the burst, tough and turgid between my teeth. Tense. Exploding.

The truth is I hated him then. Then. He pulled away to climb between my legs. Just moments before he'd said, "Not now." He'd said, "I can't and I don't want to."

I looked up into his face. I saw a little boy. Fragile, feeling. Far from me.

I kicked him. Just as he was climbing over me. I raised my knee in one swift motion, so fast and so sudden I didn't even plan it. I swear. I didn't even mean it. I don't think. He sucked back a mouthful of air and his eyes rolled back in his head. He fell over onto his side, his hands clamped over his crotch. It was almost funny. Almost. Except once he'd got his breath back, he looked at me with different eyes. His mother's eyes. Horrified, stupefied.

"What the fuck are you."

"Why the fuck did you do that."

"Get away from me."

"Get out."

When I told Daniel this story, he laughed. We laughed. He laughed like he was proud of me.

"Was that when you knew?" Daniel asked. "Was that when you knew that you liked the pain?"

"But I'm the one who hurt him. He didn't hurt me."

"Yes he did," Daniel said. "Of course he did."

And laughing again, he kissed me. "So he was your first," he said. "Your real first, on your own terms."

But was my real first really him, this boy who trusted me, this boy I hurt, who maybe hurt me? Or was it Daniel?

Or was it you?

NINE

You.
He drove a scooter, gunmetal grey, battered. He wore a leather jacket over an old black t-shirt washed pale. A smirk a touch too roguish to be sweet. The scooter had illegal plates, and the license he carried was illegal, too. Bought on the black market for the price of one of those craft beers that were now all the rage in every bar in their quiet, quasi-quaint neighbourhood.

"I'm Neven," he said, and offered his hand to his new friend's wife. His grip was crushing. Ada flinched.

"Sorry, too tight."

She grinned. "Never."

Neven was Daniel's find, a gift he'd discovered drinking alone at a dive bar after work. He presented the gift now to his wife. Watching her watch him. Watching him watch her.

"You should have some fun while you're still here," he'd said. "My wife loves meeting new people. She's a great cook too, if you're sick of the local food. We're lifers here I guess. But we know what it's like to be alone here, with the culture shock and language barriers and all those nightmares it entails. We like to take care of people. You're leaving soon, right? Well, anytime. Just give me a call. Anytime. We'll show you a good time. My wife. You'll like her."

Neven's eyes had narrowed even as he'd smiled. Nodding, taking Daniel's details. A crease in his brow as he bowed over his cell phone, exposing the smooth, vulnerable sheath of bare skin on the back and sides of his neck. There'd been a look in Neven's eyes as they'd parted, suspicious, but also curious.

He's not a fool, Daniel had thought. *But maybe that's what makes him exactly right. For her.*

And now, judging by Neven's gaze, Daniel knew that his instincts about the rogue traveller had been correct. That gaze followed Ada as she walked away, as she returned a few minutes later with their drinks pressed against her belly, holding the tall glasses in an awkward, triangular clutch. Neven's eyes flicked to and away from her, watching her go, watching her return. Fixed on her again as she sat back down to join them. His eyes slightly narrowed. Alert, intent. A predator's glare.

Not so fast, Daniel thought but didn't say, leaning back, his arms folded. *She's still mine.*

But it was good that Neven looked at her like that. Nothing if not interested. Because she had a way of interesting men, and sometimes women too. A quality that had gone a long way in helping him decide that, yes, he would marry her. If not her, who else?

Neven watched her hands, then stared at the obsidian pendant that hung from her neck. It stopped just short of the kiss of her cleavage. He looked at the obsidian and not her breasts. She was pretending not to notice this—the deliberate aversion of his gaze. Ignoring, too, the relish smoking just behind his eyes.

"Your name's Ada," he said. "That's interesting. You know, in a way our names are sort of the same."

She frowned. *Presumptuous.* She glanced at Daniel. *This clown?* But she kept her voice light. The voice she might use with a child. "The same? How so?"

"They're both palindromes. You know. They're the same backwards, forwards, reversed. The same."

"Ah," Daniel said. "I'm not sure I would've spotted that." *Reversed.*

Ada's eyes had widened. For a moment she looked shocked, but then she shook her head and smiled. A real smile, if a nervous one. "I don't think that means anything."

"It means everything. People with palindrome names have duality. We don't have such fixed personalities. We're more flexible, complex. More evolved."

"Hey!" Daniel laughed.

Neven smirked. "No offence."

They were at the bar not far from the river. They sat at one of the wooden tables outside, scarred surfaces, broken benches that rocked when they moved. Music leaked out from within, old jazz, saxophones screeching. The air was warm, the wind chill. Condensation slid down the sides of their glasses.

"At least they don't play Korean pop," Daniel said, after a pause.

Neven nodded. "*That* shit. It's all over my neighbour-hood, student-infested shithole that it is. But this area seems nice." He glanced around, then back at Ada. "I might con-sider moving."

She started. "You're not just passing through? I thought—"

Easy, Daniel thought at her. *Easy.* Though this was a rev-elation for him, too.

"Well, I'm not sure what kind of a life I'd be going back to. Work's easy to find here, the air's not as bad as everyone says, not all the time, anyway. We've got cheap living ex-penses, high pay, flexible hours…"

She nodded. "All true. But people tend to get stuck here.

You should know that. It's always just, six months, a year, and then..."

Neven lifted his shoulders. "Yeah, sure. But if I'm stuck then I'm stuck, right? For the moment I'm not sure I have any place better to be. We're all just travelling around really, aren't we? Far from where we come from. Looking for home."

Frowning, agitated, Ada fiddled with the laminate menu in front of her. It was split at the corners, hard plastic curled back.

Picked, peeled.

"This isn't home," she said. "Or if it is, God help us."

"You believe in God?"

She glared at him. "If I did it might be just to spite him. If I didn't, it might be just to piss him off."

"So that's a yes?"

"I'll keep that between me and God."

"That's a yes." He took a mouthful of beer. Swallowed. "You poor little thing. God doesn't give a shit if you spite him or not."

"We won't know that until the end, will we?"

"True. But Hell might be a nice place to visit, I think."

"We're already here," she said.

"Not a happy woman?" Neven turned to Daniel. "You should take better care of your girl."

Beneath the table, Daniel slid his hand over to Ada's leg, squeezing her knee. She lit a cigarette, blowing smoke over her shoulder. Spoiling her perfume.

"You shouldn't smoke," Neven said.

"Fuck you."

And the three of them laughed, each recognising an undertone. Blunt, brutal, beautiful. Tension shattering to finely ground glass.

Neven took another sip of his drink. "Beer is a bit dull," he said, and moved to stand. "How about a round of shots to go with it, yes?"

"Sure. How about—"

"No, no, that's not how we do it." He bumped the table as he stood, swinging his leg back over the bench. Beer spilled, glasses rang. "It's my idea, it's my choice. And it's on me."

He came back with tequila shots. Frozen glasses and wedges of lime. A grin of his own as he set them down.

TEN

I will be yours. I will be your friend when you ask me to. I will let you fuck me when you want to. I am surrendering my body as well as my soul on the one condition that you like me. That you do your best to love me.

This is what a modern marriage is. That's the deal we made. Mutual privileges, the right to wound, the right to welcome. With Daniel, though, it was also a question of welcoming wounds.

Before we were married, in the early days, I lay on his bed, on my belly, while he outlined the tattoo on my back with a razor blade. Tracing paper-fine cuts. His tongue, his saliva, the balm to my sting. Saying, "Tell me again."

Tell me again.

The story unfolding in my mind and through my words in a sleek stream of images, cool and clear, ivory and gold, like antique photographs projected on a screen. Bloodless. In spite of their blood.

"Tell me again."

Razor bite.

"I was walking home from school. He walked with me sometimes."

"Tell me."

Deeper in.

Trying not to flinch, I said, "He was taller than me. I couldn't see his face. I was trapped under him—my head was turned to the side and I was lucky for that. Because that way I could still breathe. Because otherwise he might've broken my nose. But I couldn't move. I tried to scream, I think. But I bit my tongue."

"Tell me. Faster. Tell me."

The blade moving, sliding.

"I couldn't see his face. I wanted to know what he was thinking. Was he even aware of me? But of course he was. Still, I needed to see, to know. And I couldn't. The pain, it was like a rusted pipe being shoved up me. It hurt. You can't imagine how much. I was kicking my legs. I heard that— the sound of grass tearing under my heels. Brown school shoes, with buckles. No, laces. Why do I always think they had buckles? He was breathing hard. Hard and quick, like he couldn't get enough air. Panting, that's the word. He was panting. On every inhale, his chest expanded and pressed down harder on my skull. I thought it might crack. That he might kill me just by breathing. I didn't think anything. I couldn't think. Not like that. The flesh inside me, ripping. I heard that too. I think."

"Tell me more. Tell me faster."

My blood turning cold as it slid down my spine.

"He left me like that. I lay there for hours. I don't know how long. There was metal in my mouth. Sweet, but foul. My back was covered in thorns. They'd dug into my skin where he'd stripped me. Torn my underwear off. I was angry about that. Not just about my clothes, but that nature had hurt me, too."

"Tell me again."

"It's like I was just flesh. All that talking, all those walks. And all the time, to him, I wasn't a person at all. I was just flesh. Flesh for him to take."

"Tell me again."

"I wanted to like him. I felt sorry for him. I couldn't like him. Is that why he did it? Is that why I let him get so close?"

"Don't think about his side. Tell me your side. Tell me again."

"I can't."

"Tell me."

"I can't."

But I did. I told Daniel this story again and again, until the words became a lyric of our own. Deadening the nerves I'd tied to the memory, making the words rote and their power impotent. Almost.

Later we made love. He was fucking me from behind. He grabbed a fistful of my hair and wrenched my head back. I wasn't expecting it. I screamed. The sound made him cum, the force of it so powerful it took the strength out of his legs. Collapsed against me, he caught his breath. He brushed my hair away from my ear. He said, "We are all just flesh. Every man and every woman. Flesh to take. But from now on what we take, we take together." Smiled against my ear and said, "I'm the only one who will hurt you now."

He held me close against him. His hands turned soft, stroking my skin.

Trauma, this was not. I don't think so. Do you?

ELEVEN

Daniel and Neven walked with Ada between them, their arms crossed behind her back, lashed around her waist. Tight. The streetlights spun neon red and bright white, the concrete was ballast-fire under their hard, half-stumbling steps as they veered off into the alley.

They pretended. Ada leaned her head back on a shoulder, smelling old leather and sweat raw with alcohol. She took some weight off her feet, resting back into their strength.

Bliss.

An old local couple sat in the battered lawn chairs scattered outside a noodle shop, trash waltzing around their feet in the wind. They sat hunched over their bowls, their shoulders curved under crumpled skin, their faces haggard against the cast of light and dark. It sallowed their earth-toned skin, turning it a pale lime green. The couple watched them pass with wide eyes.

"They don't approve." Ada said. "We're outraging the neighbours."

"I wouldn't worry. They're going to die soon anyway," Daniel said, and Neven laughed.

The compound was quiet. The trees that lined the drive shushed overhead, their footsteps echoed behind them.

Like we're being followed, Ada thought. And swallowed a flicker of unease.

The thin sound of a siren, far away, swelled and then faded. The standard city scream.

"I need a piss," Neven said.

"We're close, very close. You don't need to burn the flowerbeds."

Upstairs they let him go in first, throwing open the steel security door and pointing him to the bathroom.

In those minutes alone, Daniel bolted the door behind them and turned to Ada, cupping her face and then tapping her cheeks with his open palms.

"You okay? You still with us?" he whispered down to her. She nodded.

"Not too drunk?"

She shook her head, smiled.

He kissed her gently on the mouth. "Go get the stuff."

In the kitchen she retrieved the kit from its place behind the vitamin pills. She filled the syringe, her hand trembling, her fingers clawed to catch it should she shake too much. Should it fall. Nausea churned in her belly. Her head throbbed with the heavy pulse of her heart.

Yes, too much, maybe I've had too much to drink. I don't know. I think I can still think. I think...

She didn't see him standing in the doorway. Watching her fumble with the needle, the vial. She walked straight into him as she turned.

"Oh no you don't," he said, laughing – *laughing?* – catching her neatly across the shoulders and spinning her around. The syringe clattered to the floor. Her empty hand grasped at the air. She struggled but he held her tight, fury in his grip despite his laughter. Her back was tense against his chest, nerves and muscles twitching. Her heart pounded under the thick weight of his forearm. Her own hands, grappling. He dragged her out into the short passageway.

Daniel stood frozen at its mouth. He stared at them.

"Is this what you want?" Neven yelled, booting the needle away. It skittered across the smooth tile and vanished beneath the TV stand. "Is this the game you play? Huh? You want to drug me and do something to me? Is that it?"

Daniel didn't answer. He read the fury in Neven's eyes. Ada's breaths, fast and high, filled the silence.

"Is this what you want?" Neven asked again, softer. His arm still clamped against her throat, he slid his free hand down her waist, tracking the contours of her hips. His hand travelled up to the neckline of her dress and vanished beneath it, crushing her breast in a clenching fist. She winced but made no sound.

She kept her eyes on Daniel, shutting them only as Neven dropped his head and closed his teeth on her shoulder. A tear slid down her cheek, stained a murky grey from the touch of her mascara.

"She's had enough," Daniel said.

"But I haven't," Neven answered against her skin. "And I've got a feeling you haven't either."

SUMMER

TWELVE

I know what this feels like. Something new. Something wrong. Something that excites you, challenges you, scares you. Thrills you. Even as you tell yourself you don't want to do this, there's a voice that comes back: *Don't you?*

That voice. It's always there. Maybe you remember it from childhood. Scaring the tails off of lizards. Pulling the wings off of flies. Maybe something worse. I imagine you did a lot worse. The cruelty phase, they call it. You're supposed to grow out of it. Maybe nobody does. Maybe it stays beneath the surface of our thoughts, muted by "maturity." But there. When a man hits a woman, I guess it comes back to him, then. When a woman makes a man cry, I guess it comes back to her, then.

A delight in viciousness. The power we feel when we destroy.

When you open yourself to it, a part of you shatters, fragments, breaks free. A broken mirror, turning you into so many separate pieces. You see your reflection in those shards, but if you reach down to pick any of them up, they'll take your blood instead.

Pieces of you, of me.

Making us bleed.

The first time Daniel and I did it, I broke again. I broke apart like that.

But what was she? This bitchy little thing laid out on our couch. White-blonde, pale-lipped, dark-lashed. Her eyes half-shut so that when I sat by her and looked into her face I saw the crests of her irises, pale blue, red veins cracking outward in fine, static bolts.

Earlier, she'd asked me, "What do you do?"

"I'm an artist," I'd said.

And she'd laughed at me. Laughed. "Oh come on, everyone is an artist around here."

Winking at Daniel. Trying to make him complicit against me. And he'd smiled, tolerant. Only I knew that smile. Hard-eyed, blood-lit. When she turned her head he met my eyes in a black gaze.

You know, that look said. *You know what I want to do.*

In a way he did it in my own defence. In a way, that's why I agreed. Or maybe it was me, all me. Maybe it was me who wanted so badly to fuck her up. In some hidden part of my soul.

Shatter. Bleed.

"For the next four hours or so," Daniel said, checking his watch to mark the time, "she's all ours."

But I didn't know what to do with her. This body on the couch. This person we barely knew, clouding up the atmosphere. The presence of her, so thick in the sudden silence of our living room. This person we'd chosen together — or had she chosen us? She must have. Maybe. The way she smiled at Daniel, laughing in that breathy way with her shoulders back to show him her chest. Standing a little too close to him. Shutting me out. Blonde hair too bright, even under the dim bar lights.

You want to fuck my boyfriend, I thought but didn't say. *Too bad he wants to fuck you, too.*

And by the way, fuck you.

"She's beautiful, huh?"

I looked at him, my heart stabbing at my ribs. I moaned.

"No, not like that. Not like a person. She's not a person right now." Impatient with me, he shook his head. Forgiving me, he closed his arm around my shoulders. He kissed my forehead. "You're real. You understand? You're real, and she's not. She's just flesh. Just that."

Shatter. Bleed.

I wrapped my arms around him. Wanting his closeness, his warmth. He pushed me away. "What do you say we take off her clothes? Really. It's okay."

Her skin was pale, milk-white, like her hair. Her breasts were large, her nipples a faded teak, one of them placed off-centre, asymmetrical, so when I looked down at her they didn't make me think of eyes gazing back.

"Open her for me," he said.

I hesitated.

He nodded.

I touched her. Blonde hair, wiry and thick, recently trimmed. She was cold but also wet. Inside, the palest pink.

Daniel took his clothes off. He was hard as iron. Seldom so hard, even with me. Even right at the beginning, when the desperation we felt for each other had held our every nerve on high-alert. Crushing our bodies together at every spare chance. His mouth on my mouth, stealing my breath. This wasn't like that.

Nothing like that.

He climbed onto the couch, settling on his knees. He pulled her legs across his thighs. They were limp, deadweight. A fine trace of varicose veins tracked through the marbled stretch of skin just above her right knee.

Perfect. She wasn't perfect. And she wasn't real. Not real like me.

She wasn't like me.

She was not me.

"Help me," he said.

I held her for him, watching him tease his way into her in slow, careful shoves. I watched his face. I needed to see his face. His expression. Ecstasy giving over to fury as he vanished inside that cold, wet clasp. Then pounding into her so that sweat shone on his forehead and he snarled as he breathed. The couch quaking under the force.

It was over so fast. So fast, it may as well not even have happened. Maybe.

Blood in my mouth. My bitten tongue.

We cleaned her up. He let me wipe the moisture away from between her legs. Maybe then I felt the first twinge. We put her clothes back on. I straightened her hair. When she started to wake we half-carried her back down the stairs. She was groggy, moaning.

"Hey, good morning," Daniel said into her ear. "Hey, we've been trying to wake you up. You passed out on our couch. You okay?"

She tried to talk, couldn't talk. Saliva sliding down her chin. A helpless heap we dragged in our arms. We took her to the bus stop just out the alley. We settled her down, her eyes flitting against the rising light.

A local woman carrying a sack of empty bottles came by. Stared. "Crazy foreigners," she muttered under her breath, not imagining we could understand.

We waited for her to pass. The girl was moaning, trying to swallow, her belly lurching a little like she was about to be sick.

"What if she goes to the police?" I asked.

"She can't. She won't remember enough. She won't remember much about us, and she definitely won't remember where we live. What could she say? And she doesn't speak the language anyway. She'll wake up in a world of pain. She'll take a shower. She'll eat something. She'll probably call her mommy. And then she'll fly back home."

We left her there.

When we got back to our apartment I locked myself in the bathroom. I got into the shower, turned it on, sat down on the tile. I let the water crash onto my back. I hunched over the drain and threw up. I sobbed. Daniel knew better than to pound on the door, understanding me, knowing that I wouldn't know how to face it, at first. The images of what we'd done flashing against me every time I shut my eyes. Her skin, her pink, his hands crushing her breasts.

Her eyes, vacant.

Her eyes, asymmetrical.

Staring back.

When I came out again, wrapped tightly in a towel, he forced me to look at him. His eyes gentle again. Cupping my face with his soft hands. Kissing me, the light touch of his lips.

"You're real," he said. "You. You're not just flesh. Not that."

And he pulled me into his arms. When we separated I saw tears in his eyes. I saw love and gratitude. His gratitude. It was overwhelming. His love. It held us tight. I kissed his tears. Metallic, sweet.

I know what this feels like, Neven. I know how you felt when you joined with Daniel and did that to me.

THIRTEEN

They took the train out to the suburbs, their backpacks dropped between their knees, the three of them pressed together in the crush of bodies and staring eyes of the strangers that watched them — *the foreigners* — as they swept beneath the city and on to the end of the line. At each stop the passengers changed in shifting shades and varying scents. Business suits and high heels gave way to overalls and gaudy dresses; handbags and briefcases were swapped for sacks of corn and plastic carry-bags; perfume and aftershave vanished, dumbfounded, beneath the stink of sweat and dirty hair.

"Next stop, hillbilly land," Daniel said.

People, so many people, why always so many people? Push and crush and rush, standing on my feet, shoving me. Ramming me.

"She hates these crowds," Daniel said, putting his arm around Ada's shoulders, pulling her close to him. "Don't worry babe, we're getting there."

A farmer with a smart phone snapped a picture of them before the doors opened for him. Even as he stepped off onto the platform he kept glancing over his shoulder at them, gaping at them, his weathered face slack with disbelief.

"Goddammit, why?" Neven said. When he narrowed his eyes like that it was hard to tell if it was out of anger or interest. His dark eyebrows drawn tight, the crease in his brow deepened, stark. "I feel like a fish in a tank."

"Or like a monkey in a cage," said Daniel.

"Yeah, *fuck* you!" Ada yelled just before the doors slid shut.

Daniel clamped his hand over her mouth. "Be polite, honey," he said. "The one word you can be sure they all know is 'fuck.'" Then to Neven, "I told you she hates being stared at by the locals. She really hates it. Sometimes I can't even get her to leave the apartment." He took his hand away.

"It's just because you're beautiful." Neven winked at her.

She smiled at him, despite herself.

By the last few stops, the carriages were almost empty. Ada stretched out across the seats with her head in Daniel's lap, her eyes closed as he stroked her hair. When they arrived, Neven took her backpack for her. Letting her walk free.

Aboveground the place had changed its face. Away from the claustrophobic heat of the city, the fog and fumes faded to a smudged grey line only visible from higher ground, only visible when looking back. Here the roads were dirt and broken tar, and the mountains rushed up around them — vivid and green, narrow trails stuttering through the brush like broken steps made in Morse code.

They found the place that rented bicycles, presented their passports to the surly old lady who ran it and rode up into the hills. They followed the remote back roads; battered tar crumbling into wild grass, heat glinting off the handlebars and sweat sliding down their backs. Strands of Ada's hair stuck to her forehead. The guys kept ahead of her, Neven and Daniel riding abreast and talking like the heat and the sweat and the strain of the hills barely fazed them.

They threw water down their backs and over their heads, Neven turning once to shatter a spray towards Ada, an arc of flying water that hit her chest and throat, the wind cooling it on her skin, easing back her blood. She shrieked, they laughed, the sound light and high in the stillness of the hills.

They rode on, they rode up. Legs aching, skin burning.

"Here?"

Any higher and they may be seen from further down. And off this road, there were no trails. Just a gentle slope of slim trees curling around a rock face, vanishing. The ground was moist with green shadows. They got off their bikes and pushed them into the brush, laying them down so they wouldn't be visible to any passers-by, or any thieves. They walked deeper in, away from the road, out of sight. Daniel opened a bottle of warm cola, chugging a third of it down in swift, neat swallows.

"A woman's touch," Ada said, unzipping her backpack and taking out a blanket.

"And now a heathen's touch," Neven said, dropping to his knees to search his bag. He wore a black t-shirt with the sleeves ripped off. It bore the words REFUSE RESIST PURSUE PERSIST staggered across his chest in faded print. The silver crucifix he wore around his neck flashed in the sunlight. After a while he pulled the plastic sleeve out—six long-stemmed mushrooms coiled inside, the colour murky brown, the caps small and bulbous.

Like alien fingers, Ada thought, but took hers anyway. They lay back on the blanket, chewing them down, bitter chemicals vile in their mouths. Ada finished the Coke, trying to get rid of the taste.

"Let me see your tattoo again," Neven said a while later, propping himself up on one elbow to look down at Ada. Her skin was bright under the sunlight, her eyes narrowed against it. Glaring at him?

No, he decided. *Her mouth is too soft. Like she wants to smile. Like she's thinking about it.*

"Is that code for you want to fuck her?" Daniel smirked.

Neven glared at him. "No."

Ada rolled onto her belly, clawing her shirt up her back, then pulled it off over her head. She unclasped her bra without him asking. The tattoo was of a swan, wings spread, locked in flight. It travelled her shoulders, spine and lower back, shades and shadows eclipsing her skin. It disappeared beneath her jeans, and he knew it went further—much further. Though his memory was unclear on just how much.

"You've got some scars here," Neven said. He touched her without thinking about it, tracing the thin white lines that interrupted the smooth shades of ink.

"Courtesy of Daniel," she said.

"Jesus," he breathed, studying them. Stars and nicks and ragged lines. "Jesus."

"These are nothing," Daniel said. "You saw the scar under her breast."

"She at least did that to herself," Neven said. "Didn't she? But this…"

Daniel lay a hand over the left wing, blocking Neven's view. "It's not that great a tattoo anyway," he said. "A swan. A fucking *swan*."

"It's the ugly duckling," Ada said. She stared straight ahead, as if talking to the shadows in the undergrowth. "Something beautiful born from something hideous."

Neven smiled, though she couldn't see it.

"I got it when I was eighteen. I designed it myself. I saved up for months to have it done."

Daniel snorted. "You were fucking the tattoo artist."

"It's big. I needed a discount."

Neven laughed.

Daniel lay back, his arms crossed behind his head.

Ada rolled over. She undid her jeans. Neven watched her, considering. Her eyes narrowed, her mouth soft. Smiling. Almost. He slid his hand between her legs, finding his way beneath the warm, damp clasp of her underwear. He didn't ask Daniel's permission. He knew he didn't need it. Not in the games of flesh.

* * *

Daniel watched him. Neven, fucking his wife.

Fucking. It could only be that. A brutal term. An honest word.

He looked on with calm fascination, propped up on his side, plucking at the grass as Neven tore into her body. It was intense as a battle, violent, close. The guy favoured depth—frowning down at her, watching her face for signs of pain. It was hard to tell if it was fury or fascination that made him glare at her like that. It was impossible to know if her expression was of agony or ecstasy. Either, both. It didn't really matter.

She gasped for air and turned her face away, her cheeks flushed. Her hair lay wild and tangled in the grass, gleaming in the sunshine. Neven grabbed her jaw and turned her face back toward his. To kiss her? No. His eyebrows drew tighter. He paused, his hand gripping the cusp of her throat, his thumb pressed into her cheek. "Don't look away," he said, studying her eyes.

It was as much a threat as it was a request. She nodded. But there was no fear in her eyes—only a glazed light, soft and open. Like warmth. Like happiness.

A thread of anxiety unfurled in Daniel's gut. *Would it make any difference to them if I wasn't here? If I was gone?*

A gift for Ada. Neven was meant to have been that—a gift from husband to wife. Thoughtful, considerate. Something to be enjoyed and then forgotten, or broken. The loss of it something Daniel could console. But Neven was not that. He wasn't anything like that at all.

She's my wife, Daniel told himself. *Mine. Nothing that happens here changes that.*

Neven bent to bite her breast.

Harder, Daniel thought, disappointed to see tongue so quickly follow the flash of teeth. *Bite it off.*

It was a nice enough idea, but he corrected it. He liked Ada's nipples. He'd hate to see them severed. All the same, the image sent a stirring through him. He looked on, hesitant.

Why not?

Daniel pulled his shirt off over his head, self-conscious for just a moment at the comparison between himself — fine-formed, almost effeminate — and Neven, broad-shouldered, powerful. As though the three of them were each one of a gradient. Female, neuter, male.

But who is stronger, really? he thought, sliding a hand up Ada's leg so that she turned toward him. When she moved he saw a flash of silver; he saw light exploding under the surface of her skin.

Like her blood is stardust. He laughed out loud, not knowing that he had laughed. If Ada and Neven heard him, they didn't react.

The effect deepened as they moved tighter together — psychedelics trickling into their brains, making colours explode and shapes warp. Their skin smelled of sweat and chemicals. Their bodies were clammy, hot. They touched each other and thought of sulphur, of fire. Touched each other, flinched.

It was over too soon, or not soon enough. The three of them panting in a close, sweat-slick embrace. Ada between them, her head tilted back, her eyes closed against the sun.

Time lost itself in that place.

* * *

It was an hour later before Neven remembered his camera. Remembered it too late, in the dying afternoon as euphoria wore down into a heavy, dragging lethargy. It felt too close to depression, this weight. Paranoia seeping in, turning beautiful things ugly. He saw it in the moody set of Daniel's jaw, the way Ada lay on the blanket with her eyes shut tight and one arm crossed over her breasts, her free hand clawing at her hair.

He picked up the camera to take a picture of her, the beauty of her, swathed in shadow and natural light. Sensing movement, she opened her eyes and swatted the camera out of his hand before the shutter closed. Stared at him with her eyes black, fixed. She spoke, her mouth twisting around sharp words he was still too high to follow. Her face, for a moment, was monstrous. Her teeth straight and paper-thin, like an ivory razor blade shaving black words. Green and grey trickled over her skin. Moss poured out like water, washing her face in slime. This was what he saw, knowing it wasn't real, that it was a trick of his own mind. Unsettling nonetheless. When she stood and walked off into the trees to be away from him, from Daniel, he picked the camera up again. Aimed it at her back.

Snapped.

This was the picture he kept of her. Naked except for her panties, torn to a single elastic brace over her left hip. Damage done by his or Daniel's overzealous hands. Her back was dark with wet earth—like she'd fallen, like she'd been pushed. She was walking away on wounded steps, sharp stones and broken sticks digging into her soft feet. Her fists clenched at her sides, her hair tangled down her back. Her head was slightly turned, showing the curved angle of her cheek.

This picture of her was his alone. One she'd never remember him taking. And in it, she wasn't even looking at him.

FOURTEEN

L isten. You know this about me. That I welcomed evolution, that when I bit my tongue I swallowed blood. That I've never forgotten the taste. It just took me a while to discover it again. To understand what it meant. What it really meant, I mean.

That day when we met in the coffee shop by the temple. You remember it? The smell of incense smoothing the air, brightening the heat. Spiritual spice to breathe. That day we met between heaven and earth, without Daniel knowing. The first secret between us.

I got there before you. I ordered Daniel's favourite—a cappuccino with extra cocoa—knowing it would make me feel sick. Ordering it anyway as though the choice itself made him present. Like I wasn't betraying him just months into our marriage. Because of that coffee cup. His presence in its presence. Making it okay.

When I went to meet you. While I was waiting for you.

I sat by myself in the corner, drinking too fast, then not at all. Milk froth drying to a thick, fatty scum on the inside edge of the cup. I wasn't sure if it was the caffeine or the sweetness or you that made me feel so sick. Sipping, waiting.

I think it was you.

I heard your bike pull up outside. Though it could have been anyone's bike — there are so many — I knew it was yours. I felt you coming before I saw you. Before the engine stopped and the door opened, I felt each step. Your energy crashing closer to mine. And I braced myself. And I almost ran.

But that would've been worse. People like you, and me, and Daniel. We're not the ones who are supposed to run.

You weren't wearing your leather. You came in jeans and a bright green t-shirt. The wrong colour for you. I'm glad you did that, though. It gave me something else to focus on. The you that I saw in my head was different to the you I saw in front of me. Finding me. Sitting down opposite me. Ordering an Americano, thin and black. Your eyes shifting around me, over me. Neither of us asking that question. *So what are we doing here? Really.*

Because maybe we knew. Maybe we did.

You told me about that place you come from. That place I haven't seen, that place Daniel has never seen. Remote to us, sketched from movies and books and cultural clichés. Mysterious, vacuous space these images create. But then, in this country we made our home, every foreigner has this power.

We talked about these things. These ridiculous things that separate instead of bind. When I can't imagine what thicker bonds we'd need than what we already had. Blood in our mouths and thorns in my back. Daniel's hands, your hands. And me caught between.

I wanted to leave. Every minute, I thought of it. Imagining Daniel was a block away, a step away, a breath behind my ear. I was distracted, dizzy. You were losing patience with me, I know. Smiling at me anyway. Smirking? Your gaze edging round my face. It was only at the end that you looked me in the eye. Hard glare, just like his. But bloodless. Unlike his.

"Why do you do it?" you asked me.

And this was the conversation we'd been trying to have while my stomach churned and you avoided my eyes.

"Because I want to," I said. "Because it's exciting." And I smiled with all my teeth.

"That's not all of it," you said. Because you knew.

I told you about fish scales. I told you about thorns. I told you something, some things. Not everything. I told you, "Sometimes dead things move, and live things lie still." You weren't supposed to understand, but I think maybe you did.

"And you?" I asked. A polite return—but I wanted to know. I did.

"We had a pet rabbit when I was a kid," you said. "We kept it in a hutch outside."

And suddenly you were shivering, your jaw clenched, your hands twitching. "I loved that rabbit."

"But?"

"But it kept getting hurt."

"And that excited you?"

A blackness slammed into your eyes. Too much. I'd said too much. I'd pushed too hard. You looked at me like you hated me. And I knew that we were done.

We left. You said you'd take me home. I got on the back of the bike with you. My arms around your waist, feeling the strength of your body, your sweat from the summer heat. Your body already felt so familiar to me. And I leaned forward, resting my cheek on your back.

Bliss.

You took me home, took me right up to the entrance. I got off. Your eyes, I felt them watching me. Were you waiting for me to invite you up with me? I wanted to. So much. To fuck you without Daniel watching. Vanilla sex on our bed, true and desperate and real. You'd kiss me and I'd kiss you back. There'd be no blood. Not then.

But I couldn't.

And you wouldn't.

"See you around," you said. And you started the bike up again, and you didn't even hesitate. Turned, revved, vanished. Left me empty, cleaved. Like I'd cheated though we hadn't touched each other. Like we'd done something so much worse than just drink coffee and talk without talking.

You asked me why I did it, and I didn't tell you the truth.

"Because I want to," I said.

A different version of the facts.

What version did you give me, exactly? I wasn't supposed to understand, but I thought even then that I did. And I know now, yes, I did. The rabbit. The hutch. The rabbit that kept getting hurt. The rabbit you loved. Trapped. Locked away in a cage. Forgotten for days without food and water. Desperate, desolate. Gnawing at the bars.

My hands are bleeding.

FIFTEEN

He didn't tell them when he decided to move. He rode into the compound with his hiking bag on his back and a rucksack gripped between his feet. Everything he owned in the world, out here. In the East. The bike was awkward under all the weight, heavy on the turns, gravity and gradient a struggle. He bullied the handlebars, keeping the thing stable. He rode in weighed down, harried. His back soaked with sweat from the heat, the load. He rode in with his shadow chasing him.

"You go here! Go here!" the estate agent shouted to him as he rode up. He was a wiry little guy with guilelessly broken English and a thick, rubbery smile. He gesticulated to the spot where he wanted Neven to park.

Neven killed the engine.

"This everything?"

"Yes, this is everything."

"Good, good," the agent smiled. "Not so much. I help you."

The little guy snatched up the rucksack, wincing at the weight, and Neven smiled at the struggle, watching. They began the long climb up five flights of stairs to the door.

"You know," the agent said, "here we don't put elevator in building if not too tall. Maybe seven floor will have elevator. But not six."

"Well, with any luck I won't be moving again anytime soon."

"What?"

"Nothing, nothing."

The stairs were bare cement, chipped in places. The smell in the stairwell was of cooking oil and stale cigarette smoke. The walls were filthy, stamped with words Neven couldn't read and numbers he didn't understand. Most of them looked like phone numbers, but he wouldn't know who they called or what would be said on the other end. Or what to say. Were they for prostitutes? It was tantalisingly easy to imagine. Stumbling up these stairs in the early dawn hours in dizzy euphoria, money in his pocket and his key in his hand, pausing for a moment to take out his cell phone, dial one of those numbers and garble out his address to whoever answered. Pace his apartment and drink beer until the knock came at the door. Asian princess in black leather heels.

You called?

That would be nice. Except…

Except it was a cliché. An image so worn out from frequent handling that he could almost see the creases in the corners, the fading in the colours. Unreal against reality because in truth she'd probably smell like garlic and her dress wouldn't fit her properly and she'd be a little fat, maybe even a lot fat. She'd have a Hello Kitty clip in her hair and be completely oblivious to its irony. If she laughed, it'd likely be in a childish giggle, culturally trained as she was to believe it's more of a turn-on to play at being immature than it is to be sexual. And Neven would feel like a paedophile. Even if he survived these obstacles with his dick still in the game, she'd barely contain her revulsion at having to blow/fuck/strip for or be mauled by *another* foreign guy, whose sexual appetites were notorious by reputation. He would feel her reluctance like acid on her skin. No matter how much she giggled, how much she smiled. Nothing put him off more than that—the hardening of the eyes, the stiffening of the lips. Nerves flinching under his touch in tiny, tight twitches.

He preferred it the way Ada put it. *Sometimes dead things move. Sometimes live things lie still.*

And anyway, the whole fantasy was wrong. Because did prostitutes here even make house calls? Regardless, the question was irrelevant. He didn't know how to say his address yet, let alone enough language to call in a whore. No. Daniel would have to help with that kind of thing, should it come to that.

The agent had stopped in the stairwell and was pointing at the numbers, at the words. "This one for water. Your water not work, you call this, or this. This word here, it mean "water." And this, this one for electric. Problem with electric, look for this word here. Then you call. Okay?"

Neven laughed, and the agent's smile slowed for a second in confusion.

They resumed their journey up the stairs in silence.

"You very high up here. You have nice view of the rooftops," the agent said as they opened the door and stepped inside. "You very lucky. This place cheap, very cheap. In old quarter most apartment not so cheap."

That's because the place is a shithole. But the agent was right about the view, about the beauty of the historic quarter. From up here he could see right down into the alleys with their quaint scalloped roofs, murky under their film of dust and bright sunlight. It was a clear day, the pollution not dense enough to obscure the horizon, and the skyscrapers beyond the ancient city wall stood framed against the blue in distant squares. The modern sections of the city. Nightmares too far away to touch him here. He stood close to the window and looked down.

"What's that building down there?"

"Building?" The agent came over and stood close beside him, peering out.

"No, down here. Right down here. Exactly behind this building."

"That? That just old shed. Not used. Nobody use the back here now."

With his forehead pressed to the glass, only its roof was visible. An ugly square of corrugated iron, the building squat, set flat against the ground, wild grass and thick weeds rushing up around it. Vivid green.

"Your AC," the agent said, turning around to point at the units that hung precariously from the walls. "This the remote. Maybe need new batteries."

And Neven followed him, tried to listen to him, all the while with excitement itching under his skin.

This is mine now, my place now. I have my own place. I have it here, in the old quarter, just a few buildings away from theirs. But this is mine now. Mine.

He handed the agent the envelope with money. "Three months plus deposit."

Almost everything he had. His bank account gutted. For this.

The agent plopped himself down on the edge of Neven's new steel-frame bed to count it out. The bed screamed as he jostled against the hard springs, flicking through the notes, his fingers swift and efficient.

"Okay, Mr. Neven. You know we say 'happy every day' here? One day you say it in my language. But now I say in English. Wish you happy every day here, Neven! Happy every day!"

Neven was still laughing when he shut the door behind the guy, the sound of footsteps echoing back down the stairs.

The silence closed around him, alien and strange. He took a few deep breaths. Then he dug his phone out of his back pocket.

"Hey Daniel, you won't *believe* what I just did."

SIXTEEN

What Daniel couldn't do, I did.

What I couldn't do, he did.

Alone on our bed with my hands between my legs. Soft touch. My own flesh fragile and feeling, sensitive to the angle of my hips, the way I moved against myself.

"I like to watch you," he said. "I like to watch you, to understand how you understand yourself."

"Is that different to how you understand me?"

"Of course, Ada. I'm not you."

He sat in the armchair by the bed. His legs crossed so it wasn't always possible to see that he had a hand down his pants. Not until he moved. We timed it well, usually. My orgasm, his orgasm, just a few beats apart. Fluid rushing between my fingers.

"Why can't you do that with me?"

"I don't know."

Laughing at the wet patch. Still quivering. Rushing to change the sheets.

"One day I want you to squirt with me. I want you to squirt in my mouth."

A nice thing to say, I thought. Maybe some of our kinder hours together were spent like that, with me on the bed and him in that chair. Watching each other, oblivious to each other. Our focus fading in and out.

What he couldn't do, I did.

What I couldn't do, he did.

There was the day I took the train out to the forest park. It was early afternoon on a remote subway line, the carriages almost empty. My underwear damp, itching my skin because I'd left the house wet and I was still wet and I didn't know why. What was wrong with me? This energy he'd awakened.

Men. Beautiful men. Serious, sensitive. Wide shoulders, large hands. Stubble. I watched. I waited for them to lick their lips. That moment. Tongue and teeth and rasp of coarse hair. Their eyes fixed, focused. Glancing at me. Looking back at me. Staring at me. Because I was projecting something. This need. They stayed where they were, circling me in their minds. Trying to read me. Men are afraid, inherently and profoundly. Terrified. I know. And when I looked at them sometimes they looked away. Sometimes they didn't.

Hey girl, you alone?

Hey girl, where you going?

You coming with me?

Come with me.

I saw them form the sentences in their minds. Saw them stop the words, a whisper bitten mute in the backs of their mouths.

I went to the park. The forest park. I walked between the trees with my bag slung over my shoulder, my arms folded under my breasts. Small steps, tight steps. Dust dulling the leather of my shoes. No thorns. Behind me, children were screaming somewhere. Laughing or crying? I've always found it hard to tell.

I walked, desperate with the energy that twisted through me. Relaxing my shoulders, unfolding my arms. Tracing my fingers across the rough bark faces as I passed. And even this was blissful. Even this warmed me, in hidden places deep inside. The smell of tree sap, pine needles. Dead things, dry things, crushed under my feet.

No thorns. No thorns at all.

Hey little girl, wanna fuck?

This voice I sometimes heard in my head. A voice I didn't yet recognise. And I answered it with real words, soft between my teeth. Breaking.

Yes. Yes, I do. I really, really do.

Amazed, breathless, laughing. Because it was a revelation to me. A new sense of freedom. An undiscovered power, understood.

That's what Daniel did. Do you understand me? That's what he did. That.

And what about you, Neven? What did you do?

Or maybe I should ask you, what have you done?

SEVENTEEN

Her shoulders were bare. Maddening. Sculpted bone and smooth pale skin freckled by the sun. He thought of touching her. He thought of her. *Bare.*

"What the hell are you wearing, Ada?" her friend asked, laughing.

"It's the coolest thing I could think of, in this heat. I feel like I'm naked in it. I can't even wear a bra with it. Thing is, if I go to the bathroom I have to take *everything* off. See? It's one piece."

"Better make sure there's a lock on the door."

"Doors? In this place?" Ada laughed in derision. "I'll get Daniel to stand post. Or Neven."

They sat on footstools out in the street, eating cheap lamb—*Wild rat meat? Stray cat meat?*—off of sticks. The guy who ran the place worked over the coals, his shirt off, smooth skin glistening like ochre cream. He turned the meat with one hand, and with the other he waved a thick cardboard fan over the grill, dispelling smoke in fast, efficient sweeps. His thick arms were vivid with tattoos.

"Sexy." Ada nodded to him.

Her friend curled her lip. *"Him?"*

They drank beer out of litre bottles, the glass warming too quickly in the sun. The nearest restroom was the public one around the corner, the heat ripening its stench of effluent and disinfectant to a wild hum that stung the air. Almost enough to spoil it all. Almost.

Daniel and Neven sat beside each other, feet in the dust and hands behind their heads. Sweating into their palms. The heat. That summer heat. It trapped itself in the narrow alleyways, searing the tar, baking the walls. A grid of concrete coals. An urban desert maze.

Daniel turned to Neven with a tilt of the chin. "That's Jean," he said, his voice slow and just low enough to keep it between the two of them. "She and Ada have known each other for about two years now. She might leave next year though. So, maybe then. The blonde is a cousin of Natalie's; she's visiting from Canada. It's never a good idea to go for people you know, or people who know people you know. This is a big city, but in many ways it's a village really. For us. Expats. That's why it's safest to stick to the dive bars in other districts—the ones near the universities are always good. They've got Russians, Koreans...all fresh off the boat and feeling free for the first time." He licked his lips, tracking his tongue along the edges of his teeth. "Totally irresponsible. They barely know where they are themselves. So that's good. If we don't go for the ones that are leaving soon, then we look out for the single, the new, the transient. The unchained. You know."

"That's why you picked me?"

Daniel turned, stunned. The expression of surprise was feminine on his slim-jawed face. "You picked us," he said. "Don't you know that? You had a plan. I should've known it, but I didn't. You took us completely by surprise." He smiled. "And welcome."

"What about Ada? Did I take her by surprise?"

"I'd say so. She acts like she doesn't like it sometimes, but…" He stopped. "See, the first time I cut her, she climaxed. She was crying, hysterical really, but it still happened." He smiled at the memory. "There's nothing she won't find a way to tolerate. Even…learn to love. And that's good for you, too. Between the three of us, we can keep each other safe."

Safe.

Neven watched her laughing with her friends. Like any other girl, maybe. Twisting her hair up off her shoulders, smiling. Breezy and free in that thing she was wearing, a cigarette in her hand, her lipstick smudged by the heat.

"I wouldn't have been so safe if I hadn't caught her with that needle in time."

Daniel sighed. "It didn't happen like that because it wasn't supposed to. Okay? Don't think about it too much. Everything's exactly as it should be."

And Neven couldn't argue with that. Or he didn't want to argue with that. Closing the door on that part of his mind. And watching her.

Bare.

"So, we have a question for you."

Neven faced him and saw the smile there. Hard and bright. "What?"

"Are you in? I mean, are you really in. All in?"

Neven slugged back his beer. Warm, the bubbles hit his tongue in a smooth, thick froth that dried his saliva, thickened it. He swallowed and it went down in a thin, viscous slime. Not quite like semen. Not quite. "I'd need to understand what you mean by that."

"I mean I'm inviting you for dinner with us. A dinner party of three plus one."

"One?"

"Whichever *one* comes back home with us, Neven. That *one*."

Neven's hand tightened on his beer. He'd been waiting for this. Not quite hoping for it. He hadn't been able to hope exactly, not through the thick undercurrent of dread that slowed the dream, hindered it, like tarred brier catching at his ankles. Dragging him back. Here it was. His heart sprang up in his chest with a dark shudder of thrill and apprehension. He felt a pulling in his mind, the sensation almost physical. Something on the verge of splitting apart. It wasn't exactly unpleasant.

We're talking about a girl, he realised. *A girl who right now is out in the city somewhere, living her life, thinking her thoughts. A girl who doesn't know us, who we don't know. Only we know we're coming. And she doesn't.*

"Does anyone…get hurt?"

"Neven, that's almost the entire point. Flesh is flesh. Don't get that confused with anything else. That's how you go crazy. Or are you that far off base?"

"No." Neven frowned, annoyed. "I know what you mean. But for me it's a little different. I'm not sure about strangers. I think sometimes you have to really hurt a woman to make her love you. Or, to love her. I can understand that totally. In a way that's…I don't know. In a way that's really real. But with strangers…"

Why had he said that? It had been years since he'd thought along these lines. For a moment he panicked, but when he glanced at Daniel he saw that he wasn't even listening. Daniel was watching Ada talk to her friend, the barest hint of a smile at the edge of his mouth.

"But do you think…" Neven struggled to shift his tone. "Do you think it's okay? I mean, to hurt people you don't know? People you don't…you know, don't love? People who don't…ask for it?"

Daniel snorted. "Why are you so worried about people? People you don't know, you should care all the less about. Remember it. Seriously. Flesh is flesh."

And sometimes dead things move. And sometimes live things lie still.

After a moment Daniel stood, walked to Ada and bent to kiss her on the mouth. She turned into her husband's kiss. She raised her hand to clasp the back of his neck, and for a moment, her hand hooked. For a moment, her fingers hardened into claws.

Well that's love, Neven thought, watching them. He didn't notice that he was gritting his teeth. *In the fabric. That's another way, I guess. And maybe Daniel's right. Treat flesh as flesh. I guess we could. No. I guess I could.*

The sun shone on Ada's hair, turning it a bright auburn. Her lipstick, greasy in the heat, had stained Daniel's mouth. She laughed when he pulled back, wiping it off his lips with her thumb as he smiled down at her.

She understands him. She'll do anything for him.

Behind the jealousy that surged for a moment, sharp enough to make him grit his teeth, he caught a flash of something beautiful in that.

EIGHTEEN

I have a whore's heart.

I have a dark heart.

You said it. And they did, too.

Before Daniel. Before you. Long before.

I was twenty-one, fresh in my skin, new to myself just as my world was still new. I dressed in short skirts. I used too much eyeliner. I didn't know I was inviting anything. Or if the inviting was something that I wanted. Or if instead I was only walking as close to the darkness as I could get, testing it. Needing to learn where the limits were. What they were.

But you can't learn the limits of limitless things.

I worked in a bar in the city, a place still not yet far enough away from where I'd grown up. A place sunlit and sick with its own importance. The bar faced a street where the trams went by. Students and suits frequented it in equal measure. Everybody, temporary. Everyone, transient. It was the kind of place you can never lay your heart down in, because it has no identity, no core. It was just barstools and battered wood and cheap glasses that broke in the dishwasher when the water ran too hot. Guys leaning over the bar, yelling at me.

"Hey honey."

"Hey girl."

"Hey you."

Worse when the nights wore wilder, and they fell to that old dive bar tease, "Show us your tits, babe."

When they ask to see your breasts, they never call you *you*.

And I wasn't sure what to make of that. Opening the dishwasher door to a freshly broken glass, steam rising into my eyes. And I thought about how easy it would be to grab that jagged stem and slash it across a face. Puncture an eye, rupture a jugular. A spray of blood to paint my cheeks. A streak to slip into my mouth when I smiled. Something to taste.

Those were the bad nights. Those were the thoughts that exhilarated me. But it hadn't yet occurred to me to wonder why.

On the good nights the place was quiet, and the handful of regulars who were sometimes nice and sometimes weren't decided on nice and took over the music. Clearing the chairs and tables away, taking the rag out my hand.

"Come dance with us, honey."

"Come dance with us, girl."

And again, they didn't call me you. Not then.

Pulling me into the crush of their bodies, their hands sliding up under my shirt, their fingers slipping beneath my belt. And I leaned into them. I rested back against them. I didn't dance. I moved.

Bliss.

These men in their forties with their wedding bands and bad breath, their hands soft on me, brushing the hair away from my face, fingers gliding down my neck. Gentle touch.

I'll say it again. Bliss.

Joel was the one who gave me cocaine. Joked about how he cut the bar manager's grams with confectioner's sugar and still charged him full price.

"Too fucking dumb to know, the arrogant prick," he said. "But I won't give that to you, honey. This stuff is real."

Past closing time. Sitting in the front seat of his car, parked behind the bar with the night quiet hushing toward dawn. Sitting in a car with a man in his forties. A key in my nostril and his hand sliding up the inside of my leg. Telling me he liked me. Maybe liked me too much. Taking his hand away to lick his finger, to slip off his wedding band.

"Sorry, honey, it just makes me feel better sometimes."

He returned his hand. And in my head, I thought, *Why not just be honest? These cracks and desires. You're doing it anyway, so what's the difference? Why not just be real?*

Thought, but didn't say. Wish now that I'd said.

He was a big guy, too much meat for his frame. A belly trained by beer and trans fats spilling over his belt. Undoing that buckle, saying, "I just need to breathe."

And I said, "Sure."

Wanted to laugh at this pretence. But didn't. Knowing these sheathed sensitivities, and how quickly they can churn to anger. Soft hands clenching, warm eyes hardening. Big men, blistering. I knew already how scary that is. How terrifying that is. This fear they don't know how easily they instil.

"Come on, girl. We're just messing around."

He sensed the reticence in me. Said that to me, though he'd barely touched me, then.

"Here. Have another bump."

An order, not an offer. I knew by his tone. A key in my nose and a finger wriggling past my underwear, hooking the fabric back. And I flinched. His fingers were thick, scratchy. He had a habit of biting his nails, of peeling back the skin and leaving the edges in hard rags and sharp scabs. This he pressed into my sensitive flesh.

I tightened my thighs against him.

He sighed, frustrated.

"Okay, how about this then, honey? How about this?"

This was not an offer either. Not a compromise, not an act of kindness. Not quite. Which I guess was what he wanted me to believe. Reaching round past his belly, unzipping, pulling out his dick. Hard, squat stub of a thing, the head swollen and purple-tinged. The colour of ripening grapes. Turgid, sour.

At the sight of it, at the realisation of what he wanted, nausea hit my belly in a shatter-blast. My stomach lurched and I clapped a hand over my mouth.

But when I looked at him, I saw hurt in his eyes. Because he thought I was laughing. Laughing at him.

"No, no," I said. "No, I don't mean…I didn't mean…"

I was sorry for him. This sad little man with his cocaine games and his ring finger licked clean. His hand sliding off my thigh and that look in his eyes. Devastated. Because he thought I was laughing when I was trying not to throw up. And it didn't occur to me to wonder which was worse: the fact of my nausea or the assumption of my spite.

I guess I thought I owed him something.

I guess that's why I did it.

I bent across the handbrake and leaned into his lap. I brought my lips to that thick purple head. This took courage. This required a step away from myself, from the me inside of me. Shattering. A fragment falling to the floor, refracting me.

I did it for him. Because I was sorry for him. Because he was so weak that he thought I was laughing, and this was the greater insult to him. That and not the truth he didn't see.

After, he said, "Thanks, doll. Thanks, darlin'." His voice shivering, breaking. He was still breathing hard. Sighing like the air didn't hit his lungs deep enough. Doing his belt back up. Turning to me in the semi-darkness, stroking my hair away from my face as I wiped my mouth and forced myself to swallow. Chemical musk, thick on my tongue. I couldn't wait to wash it out.

"We'll do that again sometime, huh?" he said.

Said it with such certainty. Because once you open the door you're not supposed to close it right after.

"Kiss goodnight?"

Did I say that, or did he? If it was me, I guess I said it with a smirk, coquettish, turning myself into a reflection of his idea of me. My chameleon shades. Shape shift. If not that, then maybe I said it with something wounded in my voice, in my eyes. Trying to smile back at him, my mouth tight, posing as if I was about to cry. Wanting something back. I think. If I didn't say it then he did, and he said it with his hand already closing around the back of my neck. Probably he said it a little desperately, reaching for me, leaning into me.

"Kiss?"

I don't know which of us said it. Does it matter? I know that when I pressed my mouth against his, he shoved his tongue past my teeth. I know I didn't like it. That sick stench of beer and bile, the taste of his saliva too close to that of his semen. Chemical murk flooding my mouth. Again. I know I tried to pull back and he wouldn't let me, his fingers digging into the nape of my neck. That grip of his saying, *No, not yet. You don't get to leave. Not just yet.*

And I thought, *All right.*

I sucked his lower lip between my teeth. And I bit. I bit like his lip was a strip of raw flesh—which is what it was— bit like it was a leather strap and I loved the taste, like it was a delectable treat wrapped in a tough casing, and I couldn't wait to get to what was beneath. His blood burst over my tongue, a copper antidote to the poisoned taint of his other body fluids. In my mouth. This time I wanted it.

He screamed in the back of his throat, a vibration I felt in my teeth as he writhed back, trying to pull free. But I didn't let go. His fist exploded against the side of my head. He hit me so hard that for a moment I thought he'd bashed a rock against my skull. But it was only his hand, tightened, flexed.

His sad little hand bare of its wedding ring, those fingertips still spiced with my scent. Curled in, slammed against me. His own self-preservation finally kicking in.

I let go.

I grappled for the handle and popped the door open, scrambling free, stumbling away from the car. Still laughing, delirious from the cocaine, dizzy from the blow, sick on the taste.

I ran for two blocks, oblivious to the pain, my skull throbbing in a blood-burst ricochet. I was giggling between breaths. Like a lunatic unleashed. Like a schoolgirl vindicated.

When I got back to my apartment I brushed my teeth twice, three times, four. Spat pink froth and swallowed mint and blood. My blood, his blood. I didn't know.

I stared at myself in the mirror, still leering, still laughing. The wise voice behind my mind asking, *What the fuck are you doing, Ada? What the hell is this?*

Shatter. Bleed.

Maybe then I felt a thrill. You and Daniel have your own ideas. But I think maybe that was the first. My real first. I think.

NINETEEN

It took hours to find her. The girl with the bright blue halter-neck top and the over-painted eyes. Narrow-hipped, skinny, her jeans riding a half-inch too low as she leaned over the bar. Oblivious, perhaps, to the lace trim edge of her thong. It lay exposed against her bare skin like a strap, like a ragged cut. Red line through white. She was skinny, her hard contours clamped in rough denim. She wore a studded belt. Adding bravado to her bones.

They were at Blue Stream. To call the place a club was perhaps an overstatement. It was a rundown bar with Occidental dreams: cramped space, dirty corners, broken couches, stripped walls. There were loops of Christmas tinsel nailed to the bar's runner and out-dated strobe lights flashed over the small dance floor. Red, green and white stuttering against the black, slicing the darkness. Brilliance interspersed with instants of shadow, those shadows filled with moving bodies. The Christmas tinsel aside, it could have been any shitty bar in any shitty part of any city. It stank of low-grade rum and cigarette smoke. Sweat and spilled beer. Hormones, pheromones. The ether of sex.

Neven, Daniel and Ada stood at the far end of the narrow bar, cringing at the music, drinking weak gin and tonics. Pop synth and modified vocals screeched behind a relentless bass beat that no amount of cocaine could save them from. Not Daniel, not Ada. Neven leaned on the bar, one elbow propped on its sticky surface. He drank nonchalantly and he drank too fast—fitting in better with his worn jeans and faded t-shirt. Pretending to have a good time while Ada ground her teeth, crunching on ice. Daniel stood with one arm around his wife's shoulders, feeling the tension in them, feeling her twitch. There was half a gram of cocaine left in his jacket pocket. He kept his jacket on, his hand in that pocket. The tiny envelope caged in his fist like a treasure that might break if he held it too tight. He sniffed at the burn in his nostrils—the flesh there was thick and raw, threatening blood— and he tried not to think about cops. The half-worry a paranoid fault line quietly shuddering through his buzz.

But he kept it in check. And he watched.

Around them, they saw pale faces garish with overblown makeup, dirty hair gelled in place, warm bodies moving, delicate under their clothes. The music changed in shifting tempos, stuttering through varied speeds. Beneath that they heard it as a constant rush, a roar, muting their thoughts, silencing words.

But it was Neven, not Daniel, who spotted her first. The girl. Dark-haired, rail thin. She wore a blue top that left half her back bare. It reached up around the front of her shoulders in long tapers that tied behind her neck. The fabric was loose around her ribs, shifting over her insubstantial breasts.

Neven tapped Daniel's shoulder with the back of his hand.

There.

The girl had just pushed her way clear of the dance floor and was heading to the bar, hardening the angles of her shoulders to shove through the crowd, an empty glass in her hand. There was something a little like Ada about her, the way she might have been when she was just nineteen. Unmoored and underfed. Maybe this was the girl she'd almost been before. The girl she almost was.

"That one needs to eat something," Daniel said in Neven's ear. He grinned and clamped a hand on Ada's more ample ass. Ada rolled her eyes and stepped away. Her bare shoulder brushed Neven's chest. On contact she stiffened. He stepped closer.

And a secret passed between them.

The girl was at the bar now, bending further forward than she needed to. Jiggling her knee, snapping her fingers for service.

"She'll taste like fish, soft and salty," Neven said, his breath warm against Ada's neck.

Ada laughed. *Fish.* She saw rainbow-coloured scales glimmering at her feet. She shook her head, her hair tickling his throat. "No, no, she'll taste like river water. Murky. Wild."

The Blue girl took her change, her bottle of beer and disappeared back to her corner of the bar.

They watched for other options. Girls who ordered drinks for just themselves or a handful of female friends, girls who didn't have boyfriends or would-be lovers draped over them. There weren't too many of those. Time dragged on, the music shifting with it.

Bored, Ada pawed at Daniel's pockets until he surrendered the coke.

"Just a little, okay?" he said.

"I promise." She kissed his cheek, turned to kiss Neven's. Her lips pricked with stubble, she slipped back between them to find the bathroom.

"That one," Daniel said, catching Neven's attention. "She's back."

Blue girl. Her eyes roving the room, restless, leaving the section of battered and beer-stained couches by the dingy dance floor and crossing back to the bar. Back toward them. Abandoning her friends —*who was she here with?* — to get herself a shot, to look for somebody. Or just to move, to see something, or to be seen. Fiddling with her hair at the bar while she waited. Hoping she was being watched. This hope was clear in the way she fidgeted, glanced around. Leaned.

She turned her head and caught Neven's eye. He held her gaze for a second, then he looked away. His smile was small, unperturbed.

"Did you block her off?" Daniel asked in Neven's ear. An anxious hiss.

Neven shook his head. "No. I let her know I looked."

Daniel clapped him on the shoulder.

And this is how it starts.

The crowd had thinned a little and they saw where she went — to a couch that faced the dance floor, with two other girls waiting for her. These other girls — surely not *friends* — sat with their shoulders hunched, sipping their drinks. They were exquisitely out of place with their neat hairstyles and tight-set smiles. They didn't seem to be saying much.

Classmates. They had to be. Foreign language students still homesick for daddy, skimming the surface of everything around them, storing up the details of the city's eccentricities for gushy emails home. Overusing exclamation points.

> *Hi everyone!!*
>
> *Last night I went to a club with these two girls I know from class! You wouldn't believe what clubs are like here!! The place was FILTHY and the music was all at least five years old. The bartender didn't even know what a martini was! Or maybe I wasn't saying it right. This language is HARD! Then later this one girl I was with made friends with these people, and they raped her outside the*

bar! They held her against the wall and fucked her with a bottle!! Don't worry, I got home safe.
Kisses!

P.S. I can't wait to start my calligraphy class next week! I'll send you pictures soon!!

Daniel tapped this out on his phone and sent the message to Neven, who read it and burst into raucous laughter.

They watched again. Blue girl, out of place beside those two girls. Those girls, brown bread to Blue's ravenous dazzle. Pure virgin, worlds away from bare hips and brash belts.

Ada returned, loose on her feet, settling herself between her men.

The next time Blue came to the bar, she returned to her long, leaning pose, her thong riding up, her jeans riding down. A passing student—probably Russian, by the haircut—saw her and took the invitation on impulse, grabbing her from behind, clapping heavily ringed fingers on her hips.

"Hey!" She turned, outraged—not drunk enough yet to elude offence. Wrenching her hips out of his grasp, sneering back at him. A hideous twist of her mouth, bestial in the flashing lights. An expression that stripped something lovely from her face.

Neven stepped in without prompting, forgetting Ada, pushing past. "Get your hands off my girl." Posturing, combative. Even over the music, violence struck the air like static when he spoke. Lightning storms rolling in.

The Russian was just a skinny kid with a pierced lip and a torn vest. Pigeon-chested, frail, everything about him set in stark contrast to the metal in his eyes. Smouldering, staring back.

"Yeah, *fuck* off," Neven said, feigning fury so well that even the bartender, setting up a line of shooters, glanced up with practiced vigilance.

"She was—"

"No she wasn't."

Daniel unwound himself from his wife's shoulders, stepping to Neven's side. Daniel, himself skinny and seeming ineffectual. Still, the Russian kid tallied it up: two against one and the girl unwilling. He sneered and gave Neven the finger, then slunk off back into the crush.

"*Your* girl, am I?" Blue asked with an Irish lilt, turning to Neven with her hand on her hip. Already smiling at him, this presumptuous hero of hers who stood a little too close though he wasn't half as drunk as her. Though his gaze didn't waver, and hers did.

"You could be, if you wanted. How about it?" Boyish smile, only half teasing.

Her laugh was as lyrical as her voice.

Got her.

* * *

This girl. The Blue girl. Later wrapping her arms around Neven's waist, the muscles in his back tensing against her touch. Still, he didn't push her away.

Daniel made the offer and she looked at Neven, saying "Sure, okay. Yeah, why not?"

She looked at him with the promise of sex in the narrowing of her eyes. A flutter black with thick mascara. Dreaming of things with him. Dreaming of things. Of him.

Ada watched, crushing ice between her teeth.

They left just as the atmosphere in the bar roiled down to lunacy. Bleary eyes and paranoia, and boisterous, desperate aggression. Animal senses slipping past outer veneers.

"It's cunt o' clock!" Ada announced to the madness. Stepping toward the doors, crossing the bare cement floor with its cigarette butts and spills, ash and dirt, and lost liquor tracked toward the exit in the shape of her shoe prints. The last remaining patrons stumbled backwards and forwards in clumps, in knots, their arms around each other's shoulders, zigzagging like they couldn't find the door. Like they didn't want to see it, even with dawn lighting the sky a thick, electric blue. Day waking.

"You come back with us," Neven said to Blue.

An order, not a request.

Sure, okay.

Yeah, why not?

Fucking idiot.

"Don't worry, we'll take care of you," Ada said, smoke winding past her teeth as she smiled.

This promise she always made.

TWENTY

W hen Daniel was a little boy, his parents used to leave him with their neighbour when they went out. Thick woman, meat woman, low-class to his family's mid-tier dreams. She worked at the abattoir. She had a son his age. Roland. A boy with red hair, freckles, warts on his knuckles and an accent scrubbed down to such a slow, nasal drawl that it was hard to believe they were neighbours, Daniel and him. Different worlds separated by a low brick wall. The UK, a kingdom defined by accents. More so than by borders, cities, districts, maybe. But I can't say. I've only been there.

"You comin' over?"

That simple phrase made of butchered words — chopped consonants and stretched vowels — to Daniel, he was like another kind of human. When his own mother was emphatic about him not dropping his Ts, not smudging his dental fricatives. Roland didn't know the difference.

Roland threw stones at stray cats. Roland skipped school every chance he got. He stole sweets from the newsstands and stuffed them into his friends' pockets. He drew pigs in his school exercise books—plump hog behinds resplendent with starfish anuses, oval-slit vaginas, improbable penises, all drawn in emphatic blue Bic lines. Roland's laugh was a cackle so high and so raucous that Daniel, by far the more sedate, sometimes suppressed the urge to cover his ears at the sound.

Daniel was polite back then. He hadn't yet learned how to tell people when he wanted them to shut the fuck up.

But this is the story he has to tell about that. The story of his own shattering, his particular version of a shape-shift.

Friday. Roland was anxious. Skinny legs bobbing at the knees. "You comin' over?" Urgent eyes. "Friday night? My ma'am, she drinks. She drinks on Friday nights."

Friday night. That Friday night. The first Friday night he spent at the house next door. Escorted to the front door with a crush of cash in his pocket to thank Roland's mother for the trouble. Kissed and waved to and left behind.

"It's Friday. My ma'am—she drinks."

Daniel's parents drank on Fridays, too. They went to parties and sometimes they hosted parties, his mother's neck roped with opalescent beads, her hair fixed with hairspray, his father in neat suits and shiny cufflinks. Shaved cheeks and minted breath.

His parents drank too, on Friday nights. But not like this.

Roland's mother came home carrying plastic bags that clinked as she swayed on her heavy, half-circle steps. Her gait was set that way to accommodate her thighs, their turgid velocity, skin rubbing skin. She smelled of sweat and something sweet and thick—this latter, the smell of death. It's a creeping scent, one that cloisters. It coats the skin and sinks into fabric, hair. Daniel remembered it years later when he smelled it again as an adult, and that was when he finally placed it. Remembering Roland's mother. Remembering Friday night.

That night.

"Come sit with me tonight, boys?" she offered when she came in and saw them. Setting the bags down on the kitchen table, she huffed out her words, sweat on her upper lip.

"Hello, darlin' Daniel."

That upper lip of hers flattened out when she smiled at him. It turned thin and straight as it stretched and folded against her teeth. Her teeth were squat and very white, like milk teeth that had hardened in place instead of falling out and being replaced. She unpacked the bags. The wine she'd bought was Crackling. Cheap and sweet and kicking with chemical fizz. She served it to them in plastic cups, half-filled. A show of moderation. But only show.

"Come along, cheekies. Let's watch some TV. Come sit with me."

They sat at her feet watching old taped episodes of her favourite shows. Watching *Black Adder*. Watching *Only Fools and Horses*. Watching *Last of the Summer Wine*.

Last.

Summer.

Wine.

"Drink up, boys." She splashed more into their cups. Their cups kept half-full.

Daniel says the wine was too sweet, sick-sweet, but he liked it. He says the bubbles burned the back of his mouth and threatened to shoot through his nose, but he liked that, too. He says between bouts of this new delirium he felt nausea thicken in his guts. He says he fought it off, making jokes with Roland about Jean Fergusson's perplexing hairstyle, poking fun at Kathy Staff.

"You like wrinkly horse faces! That's your girlfriend!"

"That's your wife!"

"Bet you love smooching her—"

"Bet you like—"

Making kissing sounds off the backs of their hands, kicking their feet, giggling. Roland's mother laughing above them, behind them. Nudging their buttocks with her stock-inged feet. That hard toe of hers, catching the waistband of Daniel's shorts, wedging itself in the cleft of his buttocks.

"You don't want yucky old women, you two," she said. Nudging. "Not yucky old women like me. Do you?"

Daniel felt sick surprise at this thought. What a thought.

He moved away from her, from that foot. That nylon-sheathed toe. The stockings she wore were short, sock-length, the fat of her calves bulging over the reinforced hem. The bare skin there thick and puffy and pale, tinged blue. He stretched out on the carpet, flat on his belly. Out of her reach, he propped himself up on his elbows. He drained his cup.

"Come here, Danny. Let's get you some more. Roland, you rub ma'am's feet for her, okay? She's had a long day. The sort not even Peter Sallis can help with."

This, she laughed at. A joke she told to herself.

Daniel offered his cup. She filled it. Half full. Roland sat cross-legged with his mother's foot in his lap. He worked her toes, his head bowed. Not watching the television anymore. Not laughing anymore. Not smiling.

"Hey Roland, your girlfriend's back!"

"Shhh, Daniel," Roland's mother said. "The show can wait. Spending time together is better than just watching silly old TV. Don't you know?"

The way she said this, she was ecstatic, enthused. Making him complicit just with that. Her voice, her tone.

Roland's mother slipped off a stocking. Daniel only saw this because he'd reached back round for his cup, recently refilled, resting now on the carpet beside his knee.

She raised her foot and wriggled her toes against her son's mouth.

Roland bent. He pressed her big toe into his mouth. A thick bulb of flesh, the nail painted pastel pink. Roland's hair hung in his eyes, its bright red muted to a dull copper against the glare of the television.

Daniel couldn't see his eyes.

That was game one. There were many more to follow. But don't think of this as abuse. Daniel doesn't remember this as abuse. He remembers this as awkward, blissful. Scary the way it's always scary the first time you take your clothes off in front of someone new. Scary the way any moment of no return is. Exhilarating for the same reasons, and in exactly the same way. He says it was. He sees it as.

"This wasn't trauma," he says. Do you?

TWENTY-ONE

The curtains—heavy fabric, charcoal blue—were kept closed. Their living room was an intimate square space with a couch and a television, a record player. The tiled floor was alive with ornate rugs, Persian patterns and satin tassels. The passage that ran left led to the bathroom and the bedroom, and that was where Daniel went. The passage that ran right led to the kitchen and that was where Neven went. But not before he kissed the girl's neck and said to her, "Strip." Winking back at her as he walked off, playful smile and hard eyes, so that she wasn't sure if he was serious or not.

The girl looked to Ada, who was bent over the record player. Ada with her own shoulders bare. Ada with her lank indifference. Ada, older than her. Prudish? Maybe. Who the hell played *records*, anyway? Grandparents. And pretentious people. The girl was sure.

"We're collectors," Ada said, glancing back over her shoulder at the girl. "I know it's old-fashioned. Daniel and me, we like beautiful things. Old things. Music is beautiful. Vinyl makes it even better."

She placed a record onto the turntable, lowered the needle. The speakers crackled and sound followed. Electric guitars singing in a slow seesaw, a woman's voice climbing up behind them.

"Did Neven tell you to strip?" she asked. She was lowering the turntable's cover, brushing at the dust that skirted the glass. She glanced back at the girl again. "Did he?"

"Yeah." She was wary of Ada's tone — Motherly? Patronising? Comforting? — which felt as unreal as Neven's order had been.

"Well go ahead, if you want. I don't mind."

The girl's eyebrow shot up. "In front of *you?*"

Ada snorted. "Come on. We're not like that here." Something close to judgement spiked her tone.

Almost to challenge her, the girl yanked her hair over her shoulder and reached behind her neck to untie the knot of her halter neck. "Sure. I don't care either."

She peeled her shirt off. Ada watched.

"You don't have any tits," Ada said after a moment, considering the girl. Her voice was cheerful, but her eyes were flint. So sharp the girl stopped short.

"Men like them," she said, cupping her breasts in a way that may have been as much to hide them as to draw attention to them. Something wavering in her eyes, like she wasn't sure if she'd been wounded or only stung.

"That's okay." Ada smiled. "Daniel says mine are too big." And she pulled her own top down — that clasp of fabric that had left her shoulders bare all day — to show them to her. "What do you think?"

The girl swallowed, tried to smile. Ada sat down on the couch and crossed her legs under her, her hands folded in her lap. She stared at the girl, her gaze direct and unabashed.

"Well?"

"They're...very nice."

"Yes they are," Daniel said, returning to the room with a small mirror and the spare stash of cocaine. "She told you I think they're too big? She always tells people that. I've never said any such thing." He winked at Neven, who was now leaning in the mouth of the hallway. Watching over the girl's shoulder.

The girl stared at Ada's breasts. "How did you…get that scar?"

Ada looked down at her chest and traced the length of the scar with a fingertip. Soft touch. "I was playing with a knife," she said. "It's a long story."

"Ada likes to play with knives," Daniel nodded. "I try to make sure she's supervised. Not all women can be trusted with long, hard objects."

The girl laughed, abrupt and sudden. Nobody joined in. She glanced from Daniel to Ada and back again. She crossed her arms over her chest in a grip that turned her knuckles white. Clenching her shoulders. "I think…I think I…"

"No you don't," Neven said, stepping up behind her to spike her in the soft stretch below her hip. "You don't think anything."

The needle made a popping sound as it broke through her jeans. Before it reached her skin.

* * *

They lay her out on the couch, her head in Neven's lap, her arms tucked underneath her.

"Not a bad first catch," Daniel said, propping her feet up on the armrest.

Neven looked into her slack face, brushing the hair away from her forehead, considering.

She could've been…maybe. But no. She couldn't be.

Her mouth was soft, open, wet. He slid his hands to her throat and pressed his fingertips to her neck, feeling her pulse. A steady, slow throb, blood moving just beneath his touch. *His blood and her blood, separated by my mere milli-metres of skin. A living sheath. That, and nothing else.*

Ada walked to them, bent, and touched the girl's chin. "Hey, little bitch," she said, her voice low and sweet with malice.

Neven closed a hand over one of the girl's breasts. Her nipples were a light tan, larger than he might've expected. Swallowing the space. Ada placed her hand over his.

"I know what you want," Daniel spoke across to Ada, his voice low and gentle.

Ada glanced back at him, her eyes as honed now as her smile had been, and Neven felt a chill. Something surreal, slicing through his nerves. He struggled with it until her gaze shifted to him. Her eyes warm and gentle again. Her smile, returned. For him.

"Neven gets her first," she said. "He did the work. Besides," and she rose, rolling her shoulders and shaking the tension out of her arms, "he's been thinking about it all night."

TWENTY-TWO

You don't have to like it to love it. That sickening in your stomach, the sweet-metal taint to your saliva when adrenaline floods your body. Thick. Your nerves searing in a quick, molten sting so powerful and so painful you don't know if you should scream and rave it out, or instead stand perfectly still and wait for it to pass. You find the proof here that some things cannot be unseen—that nothing, ever, can be undone. And if you're really lucky, as we have always been, in it you find a new form of ecstasy. Bliss.

But I think you knew all that. I think you were waiting for it. Something inside of you was desperate to make something bleed—to see your own power manifest, to witness the irrefutable evidence of your strength. The proof of your own superiority.

You surprised me. Daniel, too. Not content with the idea of just fucking her, you had to wreck her, too. Your head between her legs, wetting her frail, dry interior with your saliva, your tongue. A fury in the flash of your teeth. Making me flinch.

Even me.

You stopped as suddenly as you'd started.

Daniel asked you, "How does she taste?"

"Bad," you said. "I think she was menstruating recently," you said.

Disgust in your voice. Also, anger. The residue on your chin was a murky brown, almost clean but not quite. Not enough. Daniel handed you a glass of wine. I handed you a tissue. You spat into the tissue. You drank the wine. That fragile crystal glass incongruous in your heavy hand.

"Fuck her for that," you said.

And we knew by your tone you didn't mean the standard kind of fuck. You set the glass down. I stared at it, innocent on the coffee table. Shining. Stem chipped. Your residue on its rim. Your saliva, tainted by her. Daniel followed my gaze. He moved over to me, wrapping his arms around me, his hands travelling my hips as he kissed my neck.

"You remember?" he asked me. "You remember that night? You remember stealing those?"

I turned into his kiss.

When you came back there was a knife in your hand. Taken from our kitchen drawer. Daniel saw it and laughed.

"Don't get blood on the couch," he said.

You dragged the coffee table back to clear the space. You grabbed the girl by the legs and pulled her into a slouch, her ass just off the floor. You knelt between her knees.

I know exactly how it went, even now, because I've replayed this in my mind many times, where it catches me somewhere between dread and arousal. Revulsion dressed in thrills. It has never lost its surreal quality.

Neven, you did this. You. With your bloodless smile, your mouth that had kissed mine, your body that had moved with mine. Rough trying to be gentle, frenzied trying to be restrained. With me. I didn't know you were capable of much else, until we saw you do this. Did this for yourself, and for

Daniel and me. Watching. Captivating us with your own idea of blood sport extremes.

Entertaining us.

Outdoing us.

You slid the knife against her, goring at her clitoris. Sawing on either side of it in swift, dogged motions. And I remembered the guy at the street stand earlier that day, the fan in his hand, flicking at the smoke. You flicked through her flesh just like that. Deft, indifferent, your wrist working as her blood pattered onto the tile.

Tap-tap.

You dropped the knife and ripped that pearl of tissue free with your fingers—pinching the tiny rag of flesh, pulling, until it snapped. A small spray of blood arced through the air, catching you across the mouth. You licked your lips. You glanced back at us where we stood watching. Dumbstruck. You didn't smile.

"Here. You want it?"

You offered the ball of flesh to Daniel, who took it, who straightened it out in his palm. It was so insubstantial in its tattered wrappings. Her blood was almost black, spreading between his fingers. I looked back at the girl who had given it to us. Unconscious. She lay still except for her hands. They twitched in fine trembles. I don't know how much she felt—if she felt anything.

Tap-tap.

She kept bleeding. She bled a lot.

You stood, straightened up. You panted out a bolt of laughter. You were trembling. You couldn't catch your breath. I met your eyes. You stared back at me, pale-faced. You still had some of her blood on her chin.

"You're going to be sick," I told you.

"I—" you started, stopped. "I think—"

You stepped off, into the bathroom. You locked the door behind you.

Alone, Daniel and I stood in silence for a moment. My throat was tight. My eyes stung. My hands shook with the flood of adrenaline.

"Did that just happen?" Daniel asked me. Awe in his voice.

"Apparently."

He poked at the thing in his palm.

"Give it to me," I said.

"Yes. Okay. Get rid of it."

He cupped his hand over my mine. It fell against my skin. Cold. Wet.

I took it into the kitchen, for a moment not sure what to do. But of course I knew what to do. I stood at the sink, ready to drop it down the drain.

"Farewell, fragile," I said.

It disappeared down that black hole. I ran the water, splashed some on my face. Goosebumps rose on my arms.

For a moment, I felt sick. Nausea quelled by the smell of blood. Metallic, sweet.

When I came back, the toilet flushed. And when you opened the door, it was me you went to. I barely glimpsed your face before you closed your arms around me, crushing me against you. I barely got to see your eyes, red like you'd been fighting tears. Like maybe you had actually cried. There was something broken in your face. But beyond it, I saw your own exhilaration masked by disbelief. You bowed your head against my neck. I felt you quivering under your shirt. I felt the need in your grip, your clenching hands. The halting jerks that shuddered through you as you breathed. I felt it. The need you had for me then, in that moment.

And I said, "Shhh."

Later we sat on the floor, on cushions we placed round the coffee table—that table you'd displaced—and did the last of the cocaine. Needing it, each of us, but giving you the most. Just the same.

On the couch behind you, the girl's blood slowed, clotted. Stopped.

"You don't have to like it to love it," Daniel said. "But you don't do it because you love it. You do it because it reminds you of something. Don't you?"

"Rabbits," you said. You wouldn't meet his eyes. "She looked a little like a rabbit. Don't you think?"

You spoke about her in the past tense. I didn't understand that, then. You held my hand. I felt it in your grip—how much you didn't want to let go. Rubbing your thumb across my knuckles in soft circles. I wanted to be alone with you in that moment. I caught myself wishing Daniel wasn't there. Maybe because I knew that this moment was important. That you'd just split yourself, cleaved yourself into a separate identity. The man who can hold a woman's hand, the man who can mutilate.

It was my hand you held. Your hand with blood under the fingernails, a tremble in your grip. Caressing my knuckles with your thumb.

Daniel was right, of course. And I understood it better when I looked at you that night. The things you love the most, you often don't like at all.

TWENTY-THREE

And then it happened again.

Neven drove his scooter through the maze of back alleys, smiling into the wind that washed his cheeks in smooth air and warm sunlight. He was getting to know the place now, learning the tread of its angles, the flippancy of its aspects. He was discovering the dead ends, making sense of the zigzags.

I live here now.

In this astounding place of filth and beauty. It was hard to believe. But more and more every day it was working its way into him, digging into his heart. The air seemed brighter, all the colours jumping in livid luminosity. He was aware of every inch of his body. His feet in their socks, his hands on the handlebars. The sweat on the back of his neck, the slippery grooves of his armpits. The hair on his legs, tickling against his jeans. All of him aware, sensing, attuned. All of him welcomed, empowered—allowed to join and be part of this world.

He took an obscure turn and found himself rounding toward the coffee shop where he'd once met Ada, the place seeming quaint today with its ornate eaves and dusty windows. He'd approached it with such hope and dread, on that day — the thick, smoke-sweet fragrance of incense tickling the back of his throat as he breathed, those breaths tight with anticipation. That smell like insidious poison. Spiritual contagion. It had seemed like that, on that day when he went to meet her, unsure of which version of her waited for him. He remembered her eyes, wide and desperate. A fragility in them he hadn't been sure how to interpret. Was it for him? This married woman he'd fucked while her husband watched. This woman who'd closed her arms around him, her legs, and he'd felt a world inside of her that went so much deeper than just that hole in her flesh.

Best not to think about it now. In a way, the lines between them had already been drawn. In his silence, in her sacrifice. Resignation like a dull film coating the surface of her eyes, desperation churning beneath. A desperation, he was beginning to think, that not even Daniel really saw.

He rode by the coffee shop now with a sense of freedom in its familiarity, greeting it as an old friend. Nodding to it as he passed, as if it could see. Its dusty eyes winked back.

He'd slept badly the night before. His dreams had been monstrous, unforgiving. Their viciousness a kind of purging — so that when he woke that morning on his rattletrap bed, his eyes had stung against the light and his head had throbbed, but a joy had sung through him nonetheless. His morning erection rose in triumph, hard as granite and pulsing with enthusiasm. His penis, at least, remained the stalwart optimist. Unperturbed, it encouraged him to follow its cue.

He'd stood at the bathroom sink and masturbated to thoughts of Ada — or the blue girl? — his knees trembling as his hand moved. Calling up images of mouths, full and soft and painted red. Sharp eyes fixed on his. Sharp eyes closed. He recalled the swell of her breasts, the feel of them in his mouth, tightening under his teeth. He didn't think of scars, or about the oily lubricant of blood between his fingertips. He blocked out the memory of plucking something that had stretched in long sinews before it snapped free, something that had almost escaped the pinch of his fingers, resisting the angles of the knife. He saw the colour red flash before his eyes, and then his semen rolled up in an electric surge. It hit the sink and he gripped the cold ceramic edge with his free hand, squeezing out the last of his cum, breathing hard, his head swimming. A smile twitching at the edges of his mouth.

A little clearer in the aftermath he now thought of Ada and the sensation he recalled was of her heat. That vital lick of energy, searing when they touched—did it come from her or from him? Or the two of them together? Like they were made of sulphur and accelerant. Like they could ignite at any moment. Her mouth on his neck, her breath in his ear. Just visualising this was enough—a maddening pulse tripped over his mind and seized his thoughts.

*Dangerous...dangerous...*he thought, knowing that no warnings could save him. Not anymore.

He reached the end of the alley, slowing to wind his way around the pedestrians that converged here. And he saw him. Crossing the main street ahead of him, his head down, his hands deep in his pockets. Daniel—his black coat surely too heavy for this heat—walking swift-stepped, sunshine beating the back of his neck.

Neven, who'd slowed at the sight of him, now sped up— the bike vibrating beneath him. Wanting to call out, *Hey!* Wanting to say, *Hey, Daniel!*

They'd go for a drink together. They'd talk. Maybe Ada would join them. It would be the three of them again, together, close. Alone.

But he was too far away, and when he reached the intersection Daniel was nowhere in sight. Neven stopped the bike and put his feet down, blinking against the glare, searching for the man in the black coat who walked with his head bowed against the sun, who kept his hands in his pockets, crushing the things he carried there. The crowd thickened, thinned, moved, thickened again. A bus tore by, a taxi blared its horn. The stillness was shattered, and Daniel was gone.

AUTUMN

TWENTY-FOUR

Walking with you, by the trees. Willows growing in regimental lines along the paved riverside. That freshly laid path littered with trash, the soil crushed solid beneath. We walked with the highway just beyond the trees to our right, the stillness of water to our left. I walked beside the water, you walked beside the trees. I walked with you. Your leather jacket, your unshaved jaw, your fatalistic fancies. You walked with me.

"Whenever anything begins," you said, "my first question always is to wonder how it's going to end."

Me too, I wanted to say but didn't. Because maybe you wouldn't have believed me—that I'd so often had the same thought. And then I said nothing for so long that you looked over at me, an edgy jerk of the head. Because you never did like to look at me directly. Not when we were outside together. Not when we were alone.

"What's up?" you asked.

This churning in my belly, this sickness deep inside of me. I wanted you to touch me. Hold my hand. Something. I peeled a strand of hair out of my mouth.

"I don't know," I said. "Something's happening to me. I feel different. Or like something wants to be different. I don't know what it is."

Struggling to articulate this sense, my shoulders so stiff the muscles ached, a throbbing behind my eyes like I wanted to cry, a shudder in my stomach like I wanted to laugh. Like I wanted to burst.

"You're safe with me, you know." You said it so softly the wind almost took the words away from me.

"I don't need to be safe." I didn't know if this was a lie or not. Not when I said it, not then. "In some ways I've avoided safety as much as possible. Almost all my life. I'm not sure I even knew I was doing it."

"Not even when you married Daniel?"

"Not even then. Maybe in some part of myself, I thought I'd be safest with him."

"Even monsters can love," you said.

And I didn't know what you were talking about anymore. Or who. That churning in my belly rising into something not unlike rage. The frustration of this endless confusion. I wrapped my arms around myself. The heat within, the chill without.

"I love autumn," you said, breathing in, opening your arms to the wind I closed myself against. "I've always loved this time of year."

What a banal thing to say. What a pointless, meaningless platitude thrown out to fill the silence.

And right there, for a minute, I came very close to hating you.

"Let's get a drink," you said. "I'm buying."

Knowing that I no longer had any money of my own. That I'd become a housewife. Which means a kept woman. Walking by the river with her fucker-never-lover while her husband slaved away in a glass tower. Making money for her.

"I have money," I said.

You gave me another one of your glances, this time with a smile. You closed your hand around my elbow. A quick squeeze. You let go. Left my heart jumping, a smile shivering on my lips.

We cut up the path and back onto the road, walking close beside each other. Easy. I breathed in the smell of your leather along with the fresh chill of the cooling air.

And right there, for a minute, I was almost happy with you.

"Coffee, or something stronger?" you asked. An invitation in your tone. Pressing me.

"No, no," I said, that sensation in my stomach ribboning to nausea. At the idea of...what? Getting drunk with you? Losing control with you? Fucking you? Or playing dead and letting you fuck me with your fingers in my mouth, my breath stopped in my throat? I didn't want that. I didn't want you. Not right then. "No. Just...coffee, I guess."

Deflated. My energy changing again. Shape-shift. This time I listened. Stopped walking. You took three full steps before you turned to see what the matter was. Frowning, irritable. Glaring at me.

"Ada, what's with you today?"

I shook my head. Feeling the need for tears again. Tears! Crying on the street while locals stared, fascinated, entertained by my emotions as if I were an exhibition piece. Unreal to them, as a foreigner in their city. An oddity. As if I was just flesh. Just that.

"I want to go home," I said. "I'm sorry, I...it's..."

I couldn't. I turned and walked back to the river, to the path that would take me home. I walked fast. You didn't follow. I knew you wouldn't. Of course you wouldn't.

When I got back to the apartment I closed the door and sat down in the hallway, hugging my legs. I couldn't decide if I should go left or right. There wasn't a single room in the place I wanted to be in. As though the entire space were poisoned. By what? By Daniel? By me?

We need to move, I thought. *Daniel and me, we need to move. We need a change. We can rent one of the courtyard houses in the suburbs. Somewhere closer to nature. I'll have a whole room to use a studio. We'll have some outside space. We'll grow things...*

Ridiculous.

It was choking me, this helpless fury. I wanted to cry but I couldn't. Needing a release I couldn't name. Nothing I said to myself was comfort enough. I don't know how long I sat there facing the front door, closed in on myself, gasping into my knees. No tears. I don't know how long it was before you knocked on the door.

You'd never come here without me and Daniel. And even among the three of us, never without a fourth. I got to my feet. I opened the door. You'd never even seen the place in daylight. I'd never seen you in this doorway with the sun shining through the dusty stairwell windows. Shaping you in silhouette.

Your glare was hard. Blood-lit.

We didn't speak.

You took a step forward. And I knew.

"No," I said. One word. The only word. A sensation rolling through me like my bones were melting, my muscles unravelling like thread off a spool. I might've collapsed, but you caught me. Your arms around me, your mouth on my neck, my jaw, my mouth. Your tongue between my teeth, forceful, thick. Until I kissed you back. And the second I did you pulled away, kicked the front door shut behind you. It slammed. An echo that thundered down the stairwell. As if someone had just left in a rage. Me, maybe.

I turned my head as you yanked at your belt. I leaned back against the wall, clawing at its surface. Grains of cheap paint gathered in dust under my fingernails. You yanked at your jeans.

I moaned. The sound escaped my throat, slow and small. I slid to the floor again, wanting to put my hands up, wanting to shield myself. Dissolving instead. A rag doll as you pulled at my clothes. I was dry as paper. I knew. You tore at my underwear. Elastic sting. You grabbed me between the legs, crushing your fingers into me. You drew your hand back. Considered. Then you spat. A thin mouthful of saliva to lubricate what I couldn't moisten by will. Doing for me what my body now refused. Taking just a few bare seconds to work the wetness in with your thumb. Not enough. Rough on soft. Then.

Climbing over me and pinning me down, your forearms trapping my shoulders, your hands in my hair, your tongue in my mouth. Total, complete. Shoving into me, my body wrenched between agony and arousal—that poison cocktail we so desperately seek. It didn't take long. Two minutes, less. Breath and motion, wordless gasps. You came so hard I felt it through your entire body. I felt it through mine.

We lay still, breathing against each other. Trembling, afraid to move. Your face pressed against my cheek.

And right there, for a minute, I thought maybe I loved you.

TWENTY-FIVE

Daniel rode the subway to work, his jacket folded in his lap, his arms wrapped around his case. Feet on the ground, the ground moving. Carrying him through darkness in a capsule of stuttering lights.

A few cars down, a child's voice lifted and looped over the cacophony of voices and squealing wheels and rattling metal. Crying or laughing? He was never sure with small children. Or with women. In both cases the sounds were often so much the same. High-pitched shrieking, needles in his ears.

He clenched his jaw, grinding his teeth. Coffee. He needed caffeine, or coke, or both. He'd slept seven hours the previous night, showered in the morning, shaved. His eyes in the misted mirror were unusually bright, alert, in spite of the dull throbs that rolled through his skull. Still, he was in better shape today than usual.

Handsome guy, he'd told himself, considering his face. And Ada came up behind him, her arms closing around his waist, kissing him between the shoulders. Her favourite place to be gentle when tenderness was what she sought.

"I'll make us dinner tonight," she said. "How's cannelloni?"

There'd been changes in her since she'd stopped working. A voracious boredom trembling in her hands. She kept the apartment spotless; she was working on her culinary skills. Experimenting with sauces, expressing herself on his plate. Her paintbrushes were dry, though. Sometimes, when he remembered to check, he went out onto her balcony studio and examined her space. The blank easels still wrapped in cellophane, the contents of her supply cupboard neatly arranged. The shelves and windowsills clear of dust, the tiled floor polished. It used to be a mess — once a month she'd get down on all fours and scrape splattered paint off the floor with a pallet knife. Her hair tied up off her neck, braless under one of his worn old t-shirts.

"Artists work best in mess," she said, laughing up at him.

His chaos girl, on her knees.

What had happened to that?

The train slowed toward the next station, brakes squealing, high enough to drown out the noise that kid was making. The train stopped, and people moved toward the doors. The baby's voice, calmer now, came closer.

Daniel looked up and saw the child in the arms of an attractive young local woman. She stood opposite Daniel, tranquil, waiting for the crush to abate once the doors slid open — a space to move through in calm and dignity as the other passengers scrambled out and onto the busy platform. Her long dark hair was clean and loose, falling to her waist in a thick, straight shimmer. She wore chic black pumps, a black leather handbag to match. Her dress was red. The baby in her arms had wide, inky eyes and plump cheeks. He looked at Daniel and those cheeks dimpled as he smiled, revealing two stubby baby teeth. The trick of lunatics and very young children — to go from screams to laughter in the space of a single breath.

"Uncle!" the baby said, reaching a chubby arm out toward him. Delighted with Daniel, somehow.

The woman turned her head and looked to where her child gestured. When she met Daniel's eyes, she smiled. A beautiful smile, perfect teeth, her elegantly made-up eyes dancing.

"Yes," she said, not imagining Daniel could understand. "That's a foreign uncle. Handsome, huh?"

She laughed and moved toward the doors, which were now open, which were now clear, her baby clasped firmly against her. She stepped off the train and sashayed into the crowd.

For a moment, Daniel couldn't breathe. His heart hammering, high and light. It was minutes before he realised he was smiling.

TWENTY-SIX

That next girl we took. Heavy girl? Hefty girl? I've never been sure of the kinder expression. We chose her for her breasts. Or Daniel did. I think. They were large and taut, perfect pockets of fat and boneless flesh, soft and warm and wet within. She had curly blonde hair, shoulder length. Liquid blue eyes. There was something a little Shirley Temple about her, I thought. Something classic. Something beautiful. Weight can work on women sometimes. It worked on her. Her clothes were stylishly loose, her shirt folded shut and tied at the front, offering a blissful view of that gorgeous cleavage, a wonder. A sight.

That girl. Shirley Temple girl. Sensual beyond her limits.

"She's going to be hell to carry back down the stairs," you said, and you laughed. I hated you then. It sounded so much like a fat-girl joke.

And I remember thinking, *You could at least respect her a little.*

Hypocrite me, I know. But it was me and only me who saw what we did to these girls as sacrifice. Sometimes I saw it like that, I mean. Just sometimes, with the ones I might've liked. That they were offered to us, inferior beings let loose among us. Led by a rope, made holy with a slit throat. But sacrifice is a ceremony. It should've been a ceremony. Something sacred. At least with her.

"I'm going to hate leaving," she said to me in the cab back to the apartment. "I've had so many wonderful experiences here."

An optimist. A glowing soul. She'd spent three years in this godforsaken place, and it had never disturbed her balance. Not the staring from the locals, not the life we live skirting the periphery of an impenetrable culture that resents our presence. As I saw it. As I understood it.

"It wears me out," I told her. "It's too insular, and too crazy. Sometimes I think it's driving me mad. Sometimes I can't even leave the house for days."

She put her hand on mine. She gave me a smile, soft with understanding. "I know," she said. "I know what you mean. But it's about how you look at it, you know? It doesn't have to disturb you if you don't let it."

This last sentence she said. I clung to it.

She liked me, I knew. There was a spark between us. A sense that we might've been friends. Maybe even lovers? The consensual kind that meets on smoother ground. She kept her hand over mine, and our fingers locked together. A promise of love in the touch. Women sense these possibilities between each other sometimes. Something passes in the slant of an eye, the warmth of a gesture. Obscure signals translated by a shared code.

Or maybe I was just imagining it. I told myself I was just imagining it. She would fly back to England and forget me. I would vanish from her memory the second the plane's wheels hit the runway on Anglo soil.

"I wish I'd met you sooner," she said, and smiled.

And I wanted to say I felt the same. But I couldn't.

Back at the apartment, she sat on our couch. I gave her a glass of wine. Rosé, lush pink leaning to red. A colour to absorb, to be absorbed by. A sweet thing with teeth. When she spotted Daniel's vinyl collection her eyes lit up and she set the glass back down on the coffee table with a sharp tap. She went to the case and started flicking through it.

"Oh, wow," she said. "Oh, wow, I didn't know you could even buy these here."

A woman after Daniel's own heart. Which was good for him, and bad for her. And I stood. Watching.

"What bra size are you?" Daniel asked. Wanting to provoke her.

But she laughed. "The size you have no hope of buying here. Living in the land of tiny tits. That's one reason why I have to go back to England, to buy new bras. The ones I brought with me are all worn out."

"Can I see?" you asked her. Wolfish, grinning, stepping in.

That smile of yours, a smirk. That twinkling in your eye, a smoulder. Something sharper in you than there used to be. Did I put that there? Did Daniel? Did we?

She raised an eyebrow at you. "The tag?" she asked. Teasing. Sweet.

I laughed. I couldn't help it. The way she was looping circles around you so effortlessly, turning that smirk into an awkward twitch.

And I saw blood behind your eyes. That dark cast in them, building. Terrible, beautiful. I put my arm around your waist. You hooked an arm over my shoulders.

"She's all right," I said. But Daniel had already vanished to the kitchen.

Was I trying to sway him? You? I don't know. I had a vision of it being different this time. Of my mouth on hers. Of her lips moving on mine. Smooth and supple skinned. A woman's mouth is so much softer than a man's. Gentle when open, full lips and velvet tongue. In my mind's eye I saw you and Daniel standing back while she and I undressed each other. Saw her and me lying together on the couch, tender touch and softer shiverings. And you could've watched. We'd have let you watch.

It might've happened like that. I think.

Daniel, back from his foray into the kitchen, came up behind her. She was bent over the records. He placed his hand on the wide arc of her back.

"You like The Cure?" he asked.

She laughed a beautiful, oblivious laugh. "There hasn't been a time in my life that The Cure hasn't been around to help me 'cure,'" she said.

Such words. She said.

And Daniel drew the needle out.

* * *

"Ada gets her first," you said. "She's been thinking about it all night."

Your gaze, unflinching. Why this hardness in you? Making something inside of me break again. Shatter. Shift.

Then.

"These tits," Daniel said. "These amazing tits. Take a look at these." Untying that chic knot, unwrapping expensive fabric. Her bra was satin, cream-white. Bursting with gleam.

My breath caught. So tight I couldn't quite snort the cocaine I'd lined up beneath my nose, where I kneeled at the coffee table. Powder drifting down to my lips like fairy dust. Something magical to help me taste. That I couldn't taste. The magical, I mean.

Magic is for dumb little girls who dream of falling down holes and don't know how deep they really go.

"Okay," I said. And I breathed in deep.

Dizzy, drifting. To her side. Climbing astride her. My weight resting safe on the soft, thick slab of her hips. Bending to her. Her slack mouth, sour. I kissed her anyway. Pulling her bra straps down her shoulders because she was too heavy to lift, and there was no other way to get to her breasts. Peeling the cups back, folding them over. Her nipples were a blissful rosé *shade*, lush pink leaning to red. A colour to absorb, to be absorbed by. Sweet things. And me with teeth.

"Easy, easy," Daniel said behind me. Watching, laughing.

The bite marks bloomed red, wet with my saliva, the marks of my teeth engraved in her skin in stuttering scarlet arcs. A torture to take pride in. I bent close to her ear.

"It doesn't have to disturb you if you don't let it," I told her. Reminded her of her words. And maybe it was wrong to laugh. I'm not sure I even meant it. But I did it anyway.

"I don't know how we'll get her in and out of her clothes," Daniel said. Daniel, practical. But also, posing. Because when I looked back at him I knew immediately what he had in mind.

"She's perfect for it," he said when he saw my face. "You know she is. Isn't that why we chose her?"

"Yes. It's why we chose her."

I bent close to her again. My hair fell over my shoulder, shielding us. I had this bare second alone with her. This moment with her. I kissed her cheek, I cupped her face. To say sorry? Or maybe to say goodbye? If I believed in those mindless platitudes, I might've said something.

But then again, what for?

"Ada can watch this," Daniel said. "Ada likes to watch me do stuff like this."

"What are we going to do?" you asked.

You said we, not you. Which I thought was telling. Including yourself in this act you could not yet comprehend.

"You ever get a girl to let you fuck her tits?" he asked you.

"Yeah…"

"This is something like that."

Nothing like that, I thought but didn't say.

Daniel fetched his neat little blade. The stiletto, fluted ivory. Antique. Bought in London when he was eighteen with all the money he could muster. He showed it to you. An open palm, a flash of silver. I saw you go cold. I saw your eyes freeze over, saw them shimmer like a pane of glass held high in a wild gale. Warping.

"Don't worry," he said. "She won't die."

No, this does not kill. This does not even maim. This damages, only. And what damage doesn't leave you with a story to tell? A new understanding of your own limits. And there are no limits to limitless things.

"She'll have a really nice scar," Daniel said. "It'll look like she had a boob job. You know? Just a small scar, right there against her ribs. Women already put plastic in their tits. What harm could a dick possibly do?"

I sat in the armchair opposite the couch, and you came to me.

"I need to sit down."

An order. A command.

"All right then."

I stood and let you take it. I sat back down in your lap.

I didn't need your permission. You sick fuck. This man I almost loved. Leaning back against your chest. Your heartbeat thrumming against my spine as Daniel bent over her, lifted her breast, tested the place. I felt the thrill coursing through you, your arms closing around me, your hands closing in, coming together between my thighs. I shifted.

Daniel's blade. Your fingers.

The blade snuck in and out, deeper, probing softness, wetness. Slack flesh spilling blood. A flash of yellow, bright as corn. The fat within. I lifted my hips, the knife came out. Daniel dropped his pants. You bit my shoulder, undid your jeans. I lowered myself onto you. Daniel eased himself into that hole he'd put in her skin, tearing it. Scarlet rush, fluid and blood, moving. Sighing. And you beneath me, within me, stabilising me with your breath warm between my shoulders, your hands tight between my legs.

A line of warm, rich blood leaked down. Beautiful as lace and just as fine. Spreading, interlocking. Your hands, my hips.

You were hugging me, I thought. Blood on my tongue, red before my eyes. Holes widening, flesh sinking. Flesh into flesh. And you, there with me. Something else for me to think about. Something holding me in place.

TWENTY-SEVEN

Ada rode the trains. Darkness, tunnels, displacement. The train was overcrowded, suffocating her with elbows and hips and bags and feet and heavy breaths. The thick syrup of humanity sick in her nose. Sweat, skin, dirty hair. And eyes on her. So many eyes. She kept her own eyes still, standing stiff between a heavy-set guy in a filthy t-shirt and a waifish young girl dressed in something that looked unnervingly like a wedding dress. Lace and long sleeves and gauzy fabric pulled tight over a bony body. The girl smelled bad, too.

I would like to rip it all off of her, Ada thought with venom. *Show her to herself. Dressed like a princess, posing for herself. Like the body beneath isn't just bones and blood and meat. That smell. Why does she smell so bad?*

Someone's backpack was pressing against her shoulders. A kid too short-sighted to think of taking it off and holding it between his knees in the crush. She felt a thick pulse of revulsion and fury. Unreason. She wanted to get out of this human straitjacket, but doing so would mean moving closer to someone else. Pushing against someone else. Being touched by someone else. Ada, clean and perfumed, her lips painted and her hands trembling on the bar over her head, felt the train rocking under her feet. She visualised destruction.

Daniel loves taking the subway. What the fuck is there to love about it? For that matter, what is there to love about anything in this city?

The train slowed toward the next station and Ada made for the door without thinking. She was still two stops away from her destination – *home!* – but it wasn't until she stepped off and came clear of the crowd that she realised she was on an unfamiliar platform.

Okay. Just take a minute, she told herself, recognising the name of the station – *not home but not far from home, not too far* – taming the panic and wondering how high over her head the sky was from here. How deep down she was. And then realised that there was no sky over her, not in this city. Just a smog-smudged dome polluted grey with weak sunlight trickling in.

Why am I here? What am I doing here? Why am I here at all?

Because Daniel had put a ring on her finger. Because Daniel had found a way to make her stay. Promising her an escape but building a different prison for her instead. And one with legal implications, too.

Oh my God. What have I done?

The thought hit her like an explosion behind her eyes. Desperate, she moved to one of the pillars and pressed her back to it, out of the way of the commuters that thronged around her. She fought her mind.

There's something behind me now. Something solid. Something keeping me in place.

With the train gone the crowd around her thinned, then gradually began again to surge. She ignored the stares directed at her.

Yes I'm foreign, but for fuck's sakes I'm a human being, too.

She moved to the end of the platform, far from the stairs,

where most people wouldn't think to board. She stood close to the edge and stared into the tunnel, waiting for the light at the head of the train to appear there in the reach of darkness.

Just two more stops and we're home, she told herself. This word *we* was used in comfort. A friend in her mind, soothing her.

By some magic trick of timing, the next train was less crowded. She took an empty seat by the doors and leant her head on her hands, her elbows on her knees. She refused to look around, studying feet instead.

Designer shoes...broken boots...sports shoes...high heels... sandals...

She wished she'd brought a book this time. Something to vanish inside of. Something to hold up to hide her face. She felt eyes on her. She knew without looking what the expressions would be. Open mouths, gaping. Glassy eyes, ogling. Even if she met those wondering gazes, the expressions on the faces wouldn't change. Wouldn't flinch. Not comprehending that she too had eyes. That she saw straight back.

They're tearing the flesh off of me, she thought. *They're eating me alive. Just by looking.*

Her skin burned, prickled.

Every place has its annoyances, Daniel often told her. *You need to keep that in mind. You can't be so sensitive.*

Still.

When she reached her stop she rose quickly and stepped off. She was on the opposite side to her exit, her wanderings at the alien platform having turned her around. But she knew where she was now. She knew where to go. She moved smartly, swiftly, her head high, her eyes on the stairs ahead. Those steps rose in a happy wall, waiting to lead her up and out.

She didn't see or sense the man behind her. A hand grabbed her shoulder from behind — a flurry of impact — and she let out a small scream, whirling round to see a young local man. He stepped away from her in chagrin and held up a phone.

My phone? For a moment she wondered if she'd dropped hers somehow and he was returning it. But no, it wasn't hers, and she realised he wanted her to read a message he'd typed on the screen.

Not imagining that if he spoke to her in his language, she might understand.

Ada read: YOU ARE BEAUTIFUL. I LOVE YOU. MAKE A FRIEND? She laughed, apologetic. Feeling sorry for this man who'd burst into her space with his opportunistic need, his trembling hand.

"No, no," she said. And smiled, offering goodwill in place of hard feelings.

She turned away from him, smiling a little to herself now, flattered in spite of herself. It would've taken him some effort, some planning, to compose that message, to have it ready.

She was almost at the stairs when he rushed up behind her again, this time his hand bumping her harder. A grab for her hip.

"You scared me," she said in his language, and he took a step back, stunned. She instantly regretted showing him that it was possible to communicate, but he didn't speak, deciding that, no, he must have heard wrong. There was no way what she said was something he could understand. Instead he held the phone up again for her to read, the gesture more forceful this time: ONE NIGHT STAND?

She stared in disbelief. "No." She waved him away, beyond amusement now, remembering the feel of his hand, that blunt force on her shoulder, that grab for her flesh.

Flesh.

"No, no, no."

Reeling, she ran up the stairs away from him, her heart thundering in a familiar panic-beat. Suddenly she was grateful for the density of the city. If he were to follow her home he would have no opportunity to attack her. Not without there being dozens of witnesses. In this way at least, she was safe.

Or maybe he was just the kind of guy who isn't afraid to push his luck.

She ran up the escalators anyway, daring to grab at the handrail, that grease-slick snake of black rubber trekking filth in a constantly revolving loop. This time she didn't think about it. Anything to get out. To get away a little faster.

She was on the street and halfway home when she realised her underwear was damp, and little licks of warm energy were ticking away at her nerves. She recognised her state of arousal with wonder. It was already way ahead of her, feeding her with images. They barrelled through her mind in blood-lit flashes, building the sensation.

A girl in a white lace dress.

A girl lying on the platform.

Strangers stepping past, oblivious.

Flesh.

Wedding fabric ripped from the girl's body, her belly cleaved, her intestines uncoiled.

Just flesh.

Thick red ribbons steaming, warm and slick, turgid.

Crushed under Ada's heel.

Ground into the ground.

Wet on hard.

Ours to take.

Friction.

Destruction.

Death.

Ours to –

When she got home, she closed the door behind her and leaned back against it, not even dropping her handbag before she reached up under her skirt and yanked her underwear down. Wetness welcomed her fingers.

TWENTY-EIGHT

I **used to walk with Daniel, too.** Do you hate me for telling you that? Am I hurting you, yet? I don't want to.
   No, wait.
I do.

You and I never talked about Daniel. Not as something that I belonged to. Not as something that belonged to me. He was your friend. He was the man I lived with. The man you shared me with when we were not together. And when we were. But alone on our walks we skirted around him, a black hole between us. The event horizon that froze us in place, stuck beside each other, no closer together and no further apart. Even as we walked together in the grey air, kicking at trash and breathing in the thick, hazy stench of polluted water.

I never told you this before. But I'll tell you about it now.

Daniel and me. He'd been here for three years, and I'd been here for three months. This was when everything around me was still strange and new. The language twisted around my tongue in knots; euphoria and incomprehension a vise around my heart, spiking me with pain and panic, crushing me with joy. And I found myself beside him. An interpreter. A translator. A man I'd met who wasn't brash, wasn't crass. Perhaps the first. Quite possibly the last. I'd snatch glances at him out the corner of my eye. His rigid profile, his hard eyes, his firm mouth. Handsome in his severe way. Mostly it was his eyes that I wanted to look at, to look into. Whenever I turned away from him, I couldn't quite remember what he looked like. His features tended to blur. As though they kept changing, shifting. As though his appearance was some trick he was playing on me, and everything about him was different the moment I took my eyes off him.

It was reason enough to keep meeting him, I guess.

He didn't take me to the river, where I took you. I found that place by myself, in time. Instead we went through the back alleys in the ancient quarter, far from the modern gleaming glass walls and trash blown streets of the district I lived in at the time. Because this was before I moved in with him. Because this was before…everything. And long before you.

"You don't know this city," he told me. "You don't know this culture—you don't know anything until you see it the way it used to be. The way it was. The way it still is, beneath the veneer."

He talked like that. Used phrases like that. "Beneath the veneer." Spoken in his smooth, crisp English, so very much the embodiment of an upper class cliché with his stiff jaw and his eyes at half-mast. So much like this that I sometimes had to work hard not to laugh at him. I stopped myself because I had a sense that if I did, he might do something. Hit me, maybe. There always was the threat of violence in the way he kept his hands jammed in his pockets. Clenched, hidden. Not like you, who kept yours free, in plain sight.

You, at least, were always more direct about your malice. More honest, in some ways, about your desire to do harm.

For the first serious date he took me on, we went to the barbecue street. That famous place. Another tourist trap. I wore a sleek red bodice, a black lace bra. Blue jeans. My hair clipped up in a French barrette. It was the first time I dressed up for him. Lipstick greasy on my mouth, my perfume at war with my sweat. It was summer, hot. There was fire there. Lots of it. And crowds of people thronged between the rows of stalls. Shoulders and heads and slow-stepping feet. Smoke thick in the air, the smells of spice and meat and things not meat. Everything, roasting. Young men with cardboard fans and close-shaved heads worked over the coals, waving back the smoke, turning kebabs. Crowds pushed backwards and forwards with skewers in their hands. Eating incredible things. Dropping the sticks. Spikes under my feet.

I told myself, *Not thorns.*

On this street they roasted scorpions, snakes, frogs. Silk-worms, beetles, cicadas. Innards, testicles, eyeballs. All the imaginable parts not meat. The unimaginable parts, too.

Daniel and I bought plastic cups of beer from vendors. It spilled easily, froth slipping over the edge in a slow, sticky slide. None of the cups were ever quite cold enough. We gulped it back; we drank too fast. I worried where the bathrooms were. Remembered that the public restrooms in this place were all holes in the ground, clamped in aluminium, the tile splashed with urine turned brown from the filth brought in by shuffling feet. Stepping in it. I wasn't used to that yet.

I told myself, *Wait.*

We wandered deeper down that thick, moving street. Crush and rush and incredible heat. We stopped at a larger stall, one decked out with labels written in English. American tourists gaggling, gawking. Daniel dragged me past them. He led me by the hand.

"Now this is worth taking a picture of," he said, laughing.

They specialised in phalli. Horse, donkey, pig, cow. Even chicken, tiny and pink, skewered together so that each stick looked like some sort of sea-creature. Tendrils and rubbery tips, soft and raw.

One of the guys working the coals caught my eye, my wonderstruck expression. He smirked at me from behind his stall. Yelled to me in English, "You want some penis?"

Laughing when I laughed. Winking at me.

But then Daniel's arm closed around my shoulder. "Do you? I'll buy it for you."

Awkward. He was trying too hard. Spoiling the joke, I thought. But now, looking back, it's possible that he was sincere. That he wanted to watch me eat a phallus. To see how I looked, tearing at it with my teeth.

I shook my head. Smiled an apology to the guy at the coals. We moved on. We ate kidneys instead. Heavily spiced, rich, the texture dense and thick. I ate a row of chicken hearts. Tense little purses of tough flesh, squirting in my mouth, blood leaking down my chin. I wiped it off with the back of my hand.

He watched.

"I'm coming back with you tonight," he said.

And I laughed. "No you're not."

"I want to see your art," he said.

I still don't know why I agreed to that. I believed him, I think. Maybe it was that.

* * *

He walked with me. He wanted to see my paintings. My personal take on disassembling form. He wanted to know which parts I chose to see. Or forced myself to see. I interested him like that. But not you. That's where you and Daniel always differed. You were blunt, direct, a lead pipe smashed over the head. And Daniel was nothing if not dense with subtleties.

And so he came back with me that night. And I showed him.

A woman's breast in transection. Fat and skin and fine layers of tissue. I used purple, indigo, blue. The gland within a florid green. Something rancid, rotting beneath the surface. Something you'd have to slice into to see.

A vivid blue eye with a violent red pupil. Exploding tears. Fanciful tadpoles, spermatozoa swimming. Spinning.

A parking lot, dark, a woman standing under a streetlamp. Faceless in miniature. I did that in pen and ink, of course. I knew there was no brightness in that place. I remembered it too well.

A watercolour of a flat field, a path for one cutting through. Crushed by two. That empty landscape filled with thorns, grass glowing wheat-yellow under a toxic summer sun. Two blades of grass painted red. Shining wet. This I saw without remembering. This I remembered without the need for sight.

I'd spent hours on these pieces. With each one, no matter the subject, I was sketching myself. I knew that, and I did it anyway. Recreating pieces of me. Disassembled. Broken. Fragments that cut into me as I handled them. Sharp shards. I examined them anyway. Because long ago I'd developed this habit, the one where I practice taking myself apart.

"You don't have to keep revisiting these things," Daniel told me.

Daniel. Still strange to me then. So crisp and clean against the muddled culture I'd once called mine. So different to the men I'd been with before, in all the places I'd travelled to. He stalked my new apartment, a cat sniffing at the corners. A man in a smart jacket, impeccably shaved, cologned, stiff under his skin. Red-eyed from all that beer, the smell of smoke still trapped in his clothes. He surveyed the canvases it had cost the last of my savings to ensure I could bring with me. They were lined up around my bedroom, leant against radiators, propped against the walls. An inchoate, stuttering series of images. Each of them an aspect of me. I stood fully clothed. I stood just behind him. I stood and trembled as if I was naked. As though I was cold.

The room smelled of me. Sweat, perfume. The prince bed was conspicuous behind us. That afternoon, before I went to meet him, I'd taken a shower and then tried to sleep. The pillows were still damp from my hair. There may or may not have been a circle of moisture on the mattress, because before I'd given up on sleep, I'd wrenched an orgasm out of myself. A rabid hunger, barely fed. I worried that he knew, somehow.

Now I know he knew, of course. Daniel always had a nose for sex.

Remember this, before you panic: he came to me.

Or, I let him come to me.

"There's history here, isn't there?" He said that on his knees, bending to inspect the art I'd created in the life I'd left behind. A life that just a few months before had been my reality, and now was already only memory, remote, surreal. A different version of myself. He was staring at a yellow field. Raising a hand and pointing a finger to touch a blade of grass I'd dabbed red.

"Isn't there?" he asked.

I folded my arms, glaring down at him. "It's just a field," I said. My voice low to keep it steady. My shoulders were shaking. I locked my muscles and prayed he wouldn't notice.

He looked up at me. His smile hard, blood lit. His eyes, soft. "Don't play," he told me. "This isn't a game."

He stood. He stared down at me until I looked away. Then he took my face in his hands, his index fingers pressing into the hollow past my jaw, below my ears. The barest hint of a threat, with those hard digits not quite digging into the soft flesh that sheathed my salivary glands. I tasted kidneys, hearts. I tasted blood. He made me look up.

"No, I don't want to play with you," he said. "Not you, I don't think."

And he did at last what I'd been waiting for him to try for weeks. He kissed me.

That first time, he was gentle. I was the one who wanted to bite.

TWENTY-NINE

The day was blustery, dark. The sky was clouded with thick fumes that plumed from the smokestacks. Coal burning all across the city, choking the air. They walked through it anyway, Neven and Ada, side by side. Not touching. Their hands passing inches apart as they stepped.

"We should really buy gas masks," she said. "This stuff is probably killing us. All of us. An entire city wiped out by toxic air. And everybody knows about it. And nobody gives a shit."

"When did you last see a full week of blue sky?"

"Here?" She snorted, shook her head. "Never, I don't think."

Never.

The word was so final that Neven felt a sinking in his gut, a dizzy terror at what he'd handed himself over to. *I've moved here now. I'm stuck here now. Could I leave as easily as I came?* And right behind this, he thought, *What the fuck have I done?*

"Daniel wants to have a baby."

Ada spoke so quietly, so simply, that for a moment Neven didn't respond, piecing the sounds together in his mind until they formed themselves into a kind of sense. "What?"

"Daniel. He wants—"

Neven reeled. *"What?"*

Ada stopped, waited for him to turn and look at her. When he did she held her arms out in a helpless gesture. Her smile saying, *What can I do?*

His hands hovered at her shoulders. To push her? To grab onto her?

"Well, tell him *no*. Tell him you can't do that. It's your choice too, you know."

She folded her arms and lifted her shoulders in a small shrug. "I know. But see, he saw this woman and her baby on the subway the other day—"

"Some woman? He saw some woman and his whole world got turned around? His entire fucking—"

"No, no, listen. The way he described her to me, you have no idea. It was so beautiful. He says she was—"

"So he told you some fucking fairy story about some babe neither of you know, some woman and her *whelp*, and now you want to be a mommy? You? With him? You *and him?*"

"I'd be a good mother."

"Like hell. Like *hell*, Ada. Christ. What are you thinking?"

Like hell. Words like cannonballs exploding the ground under her feet. Words licked with sulphur and suffused with arsenic. Sweat burst on the back of Ada's neck. Her hands fisted. "You don't have to be such an asshole you know," she said. "You don't have to treat me like—"

"I'll treat you however the fuck I want. You *ask* for that. No?"

"No," she moaned and closed her eyes, her brow furrowed against an emotion that might, maybe, have been rage. "No, I don't ask for that. Nobody asks for that."

"You know what, Ada? You deserve exactly what you get." Sneering against the pain in his eyes. *"Exactly* what you fucking get. I hope he kills someone one day. I hope *you* kill someone one day. Fuck it, I hope he kills *you. Both* of you."

"He'd never do that," she said quietly. "He married me. And our child—"

"Your *child*?"

"Yes, Neven. You don't understand. Daniel and me, no matter what, see, he and I are partners—"

"Yeah, well, *keep* it." He spat on the ground at her feet. He didn't look at her again.

Watching him walk away, Ada closed her hands over her stomach, her fingers interlocked, pressing. Her breaths so tight that dizziness caught her, and she wasn't sure what it was that made the world spin so suddenly: his glare, his saliva, the tearing inside of her. Or maybe it was the sky—just that—a hard grey wall locked over her head, blocking out the light.

THIRTY

But how could we stay away? With so many bridges forged, so many lines crossed?

It sounds stupid. Trite. Cliché. That we crossed lines together. That we made bonds between the breaks. But it's true. It's true. It is.

Even after you walked away, Daniel fucked me and I dreamed of you. Understanding the irreparable difference between us as I did, I thought about it anyway. Biting his shoulder, reimagining his dimensions. Him like a needle, you like a punch. I sought satisfaction in the dream and not the truth.

I dreamed of you.

That insincere platitude: "let's just be friends." Poisonous. Trite. A line they say in movies, on TV shows. A line all the liars say.

So we made ourselves liars. We turned ourselves inside out and hid behind the insincere. Proximity biting. Anything to keep seeing you.

Anything to—

WINTER

THIRTY-ONE

When the next sighting came, it didn't go unnoticed. When the next sighting came, they laughed.

Neven was at the front door getting ready to leave. He was wrapping his scarf around his neck in slow strokes, his boots still unlaced, his jacket hanging open. He took his time getting ready, fiddling with wool and trying to think of things to say. A bitter taste tainted the back of his mouth. His eyes smarted as though singed with smoke.

It was violent, this tension.

Ada and Daniel watched, standing close together, waiting. Avoiding Neven's eyes. Ada's jaws were clenched behind her smile, and every nerve in her body rang tight as piano wire. Daniel posed beside her with his hand pressed to the small of his wife's back. Instead of smiling, he kept his eyes on Neven's bootlaces. Long and brown to match the leather, still damp with melted snow.

Dirty, Daniel thought.

Then Neven stopped, his eyes brightening like a light had just gone on, his hands frozen at his collar where he was still arranging his scarf. "By the way," he said to Ada, "sorry for nearly running you over yesterday."

She raised an eyebrow at him. "Running me over?"

"It *was* you, wasn't it?"

"I don't think so," she said. "Yesterday? I don't think I went out yesterday." She glanced at Daniel and folded her arms under her breasts. She held her shoulders high, drawn in. "Did I?"

"No. I went out in the afternoon, but Ada was home all day." Daniel's face relaxed into his easy smile, and he clapped his friend on the shoulder. "Who is this girl that looks like my wife, and why are you trying to kill her?"

They laughed, or tried to—deferential, awful.

And Neven thought, *Breathe.*

It was evening's end. The food had been eaten, the wine drunk, the music stopped. They'd listened to Daniel's old Dead Can Dance LPs during the meal, the silence between tracks broken by chewing sounds, swallowing sounds— gulping sounds when Neven drank too fast, hoping it would encourage his hosts to produce more wine. Ada's laughter subdued to a sharp titter, the sound oddly stiff, like starched sheets snapping in a high wind. When the wine was gone and no more offered, they drank coffee and talked about movies they wanted to see, records they wanted to buy. Safe topics. Polite. Surreal when he compared the *safe* and the *po-lite* to what the three of them had been. In that other life.

Just three months ago, there would be none of this raw silence. The dining room table would be strewn with rolled up paper money and a few bloody tissues along with the crumpled napkins and splashes of spilled sauce. They would be drunk by now, drunk and high and insensible. Blissful. Music growling in low, smoky tones, and never anything as pseudo-soulful as Dead Can Dance, which he'd never exactly swooned over.

Didn't I nearly run you over yesterday, Ada? Didn't I almost ride right over you?

At this hour Daniel would be taking out the stash, cracking black jokes as Ada cracked open another bottle of wine. They'd be snorting white powder until Ada's nose started to bleed. They'd stretch her out on the couch, her eyes softening to slits as the room spun around her. Daniel going to her from time to time to brush the hair from her face, to kiss her forehead.

Smiling back at Neven. *How's our girl tonight, huh?*

And she'd reach her arms out to him, to them.

Now Ada's eyes were wide and wary above that stiff smile. And Daniel hid behind his role of host—host as tolerator, guest as invader.

Guest, Neven thought. *That's what I am now to him. To them. How did this happen? Or really…why?*

He thought friendships were always safe, once they became real and raw and rooted in the quick, nesting in the fibres of the soul. As his friendship with Daniel and Ada used to be. Now he stood stuck in their hallway, strangling himself with musty fabric, all the hungers above and below his belly left unfed. Nauseous on Ada's cream sauce, always too rich. His dick pressed hard against his zip, throbbing so it hurt.

"I could *swear* it was you," he said to Ada. "You were wearing that red leather coat of yours. I went by on my Vespa and had to swerve—I nearly knocked you over."

She glanced up at Daniel, then back to him. "I must have a doppelganger," she said, and laughed—a wild sound, too loud, too explosive. It made both men flinch. Ada's laughter stopped in her throat. Something twisted and burned in the new silence.

This is gone, Neven thought, hating their tight hallway, their awkward faces, the nest of laces tangled round his feet. *I guess this is dead.*

Right now leaving would be a relief, but he knew it would hurt later, once he arrived home sober and alone, half-desperate with arousal, confused and displaced.

Neven laced his boots, closed his jacket. He kissed them both goodbye in a series of awkward pecks. Ballast fire on flinching skin.

The moment his back was turned, the door shut and the lock clicked home behind him.

* * *

Outside, Neven walked the strip of chill darkness back to his own apartment, just a few buildings down from theirs. A proximity they'd once treasured; one they were sure to dread in time. Fresh snow squeaked under his boots, a feather fall that numbed his cheeks and clung to his eyelashes, blurring everything to a soft white sparkle. He trudged through it without seeing it or feeling it. He was replaying that moment on the bike. The flash of light in his eyes as he rounded the cor-ner — sunshine glancing off a shop window, a blade slashing his vision. The feel of the back wheel sliding out from under him. The swerve to correct it — just a sway, very slight — his shoulder and arm muscles tensing as he bullied the machine back under control. And then there was the girl — *Ada!* Her name had flashed through his head like a scream in song — stumbling back, snapping round to look at him. Her eyes wide and startled and very blue in that crystal light. Her eyebrows swept high in surprise, the edge of her coat swirling as she stumble-stepped clear of his path.

He'd lifted the fingers of his left hand to her as he whipped by. He'd wanted to shout something to her over his shoulder, but he passed too quickly and his heart was still shudder-thudding from the brush, a burst of adrenaline wild in his blood. Then she was behind him, and he was at the end of the street. And he was turning the bike into traffic. And it was past.

I'll send her a message later, he'd thought. *Maybe even make a joke of it.*

It was an excuse to get back in touch, to contact her personally, to share something with her, even if it was a near-accident. But somehow he'd forgotten about it until that last moment at the end of the night. Dinner with Daniel and Ada. Dinner at Daniel and Ada's. *With* and *at* now worlds apart. There was no *with* anymore in their dark little apartment where so much was the same, and everything had changed.

"I must have a doppelganger." Ada had laughed. Her sudden, sharp smile a knife edge that almost hurt him. The eyes above the smile watchful, wondering.

That girl on the street, she looked just like her. Like she did before. But of course it was her. Whatever she says. It was.

When he reached his own door the snow had stopped and the wind had stilled. Heading up the stairs, the echo of his footsteps followed close behind him.

* * *

As Neven brushed his teeth and stared at his face in the mirror — eyes less bloodshot, no less hollow — Ada lay on her belly while Daniel traced his fingers across her back.

"It'll look like shit eventually," Daniel said, outlining the swan's neck, the starburst flower patterns that flew from its wings and scattered at her shoulders. Touching the scars he'd made. "When you're older, you know, and your skin starts to loosen."

"It's easy to hide at least," she said.

"Not if we go swimming."

She sighed, a frustrated hiss of breath. "I'll swim in a t-shirt then, okay?"

He bent to kiss the space between her shoulder blades, the scars he had not made, the places where the needle had dug too deep. An amateur tattoo artist. A fantasy tattoo. The kind you think will last forever when you're young and cannot imagine yourself aged. The touch of his lips tickled. She twitched, teeth clenched.

"Just relax," he said, sliding a hand down her spine and over her buttocks, his hand disappearing in the hollow between her legs. His fingers teased at the warm, moist slit that travelled there. "You want this, don't you?"

I want this, she told herself.

"Don't you?"

She shifted, propped herself up on her elbows, put her head in her hands. "Yes," she said into her open palms. Her voice was muffled. "I do."

I do.

THIRTY-TWO

Ada. Listen. What did you ever know about me?

Everything I needed to know I learned in the house where I grew up. I learned it before you. I learned it differently from you. I think I learned it better, too. You and Daniel, so smug and secure in your sick little world. You did it safely, do you know that? Of course not. You married that pretentious fuck. He made you pretentious, too. You wouldn't know true brutality if I tied you to a chair and cut your tits off, gouged your eyes out. Rammed a poker up your cunt. Fucked you with it until I punctured both your lungs. Kissed the blood as you choked it past your lips. I thought about doing that, you know. Toward the end, when you made me mad. And later, again, when you broke my heart. If for no other reason than to watch the surprise twist past the agony in your face. Even at the beginning, I sometimes fantasised about doing that to you because you were suffocating me with your assumptions, your impressions. All the things you were so sure you knew about me. And later I wanted to do it because I knew you felt sorry for me.

Fuck you.

And while you're at it, ask yourself this: what did I ever really talk to you about? What did I ever tell you in plain words? About myself. About what I thought of you.

Nothing.

But I did always like your inconsistencies. Your contradictions. The one thing that I'll admit truly intrigued me about you.

It was a reason to keep meeting with you, at least.

Even monsters can love. I told you that. I also told you that you were safe with me.

Well, are you?

Would you be?

What do you think?

While you're thinking, remember this: you're not safe with him, either.

You shouldn't have cut me off, Ada. I'm the only person in the world who gets you. I know what you need. Better than you do.

THIRTY-THREE

Three days after the dinner party, Daniel went to the coffee shop near his office. It hadn't snowed much more since that night, and what was left of the light fall was grey and black with street filth, frozen and melted in turns, churned to a thin layer of slush in the gutters. The air was sharp but he pulled his scarf away from his mouth, breathing it in to wake himself up.

Fatigue hummed in the nerves that ran across his scalp. A constant vibration urging him to lower his head, to sleep, to rest for a few minutes.

Coffee, he thought. He was supposed to be cutting back, but Ada wasn't here to see, to stop him, to judge him in that spiked-saccharine way of hers that made him think of barbs embedded in sweets. Bite, and expect to be bitten. Ada wasn't here. She was at home in their apartment cat-napping on the couch with the TV on low. She was home, and if he didn't have some coffee he would fall asleep at his desk, or risk dozing through his meeting that afternoon. His boss and colleagues picking apart project details in low, focused tones. The pattern of their voices reminding him of meditation tapes, that soft, indecipherable buzz. His eyelids drooping until he slipped his hands under the desk, flicked his lighter and held a hand over the flame, finding focus in the burn. Blistering his palms.

Coffee. Wake up.

A double shot, large cappuccino, extra chocolate on the foam to satisfy his sweet tooth. It would be rich. It might unsettle his stomach, but that would just be another thing to keep him on his toes, wouldn't it?

He pushed open the doors of Double Cream, the bell over his head tinkling. He walked straight past the display fridges with their staggering triple-tier cakes, sold by the slice, each in various stages of demolition. At the counter, a young guy with a wispy attempt at a beard looked at him in surprise. Then greeted him in slangy city speech.

That's different, Daniel thought. He was expecting a stream of broken English offered with a hopeful smile, followed by visible relief when Daniel replied to show that yes, he could in fact speak the language.

Daniel fumbled in his coat for his wallet. "Large cappuccino, double shot—"

"—Extra cocoa powder. I remember. Did you drop it?"

Daniel stopped, frowned. "What?"

"Your coffee. Did you drop it outside? If you'd dropped it in-store I coulda replaced it free, but if you didn't—and I'm pretty sure you didn't—I'm afraid I'll have to charge you again. Sorry, brother."

"What do you mean? What are you talking about?"

The kid rolled his eyes. "Look friend, I can't give you another one for free just like that. You didn't drop it in-store. I can't replace it. You're gonna have to buy another one."

"That's—that's what I want," Daniel said, irritated. "I would like to *buy* a cappuccino, double shot—"

"And you want lots of cocoa. Yeah, okay, okay."

The kid shouted the order over his shoulder to the guys at the coffee machines. One of them—a big man with a tattoo on his neck—spotted Daniel and did a sharp double-take. He gave Daniel a brief, perplexed stare. The kid at the bar took Daniel's money, gave him his change without thanks. The kid's fingers were greasy, the nails bitten to the quick in luminous arcs, sensitive flesh semi-healed to a bright pink that still remembered blood.

I coulda replaced it free —

I'll have to charge you again —

Daniel stood back with his hands in his coat pockets, agitated, watching.

Hot air hissed through milk.

A woman and a little girl came in, holding hands. The child dragged her mother to the display fridges, her chubby finger smearing the glass as she pointed out a cake.

"There! This one! There!"

Daniel watched them, unconscious of the vacant cast of his face as other patrons looked on and smiled. He looked haggard, hollow, shadows pressed under his eyes. In his pockets, his fists clenched and unclenched. The mother glanced his way, her smile hardening as she pulled her daughter closer to her. She looked deliberately away.

She thinks I'm a predator, he thought, waking up. *Some monster who would —*

"Hey, friend."

Daniel didn't hear him.

"Hey, cappuccino man. *Hello!*"

The kid had half-stepped out from behind the counter and was pointing to the cappuccino, capped and waiting in a takeaway cup.

It occurred to Daniel he hadn't specified that he wanted it to go. He did, of course. But—

"Sure, coming."

As he passed the counter again on his way out, he paused. "Sorry...kid?"

The kid flinched at the title, sarcasm twitching at the edges of his mouth as he smiled. "Yeah? You want another one already?"

"Did...did you say I ordered one of these before?"

"Uh, *yeah*. You did. About ten minutes before you came back in now."

Daniel took a sip of the coffee. It was too hot and the first drop touched the tip of his tongue like a piercing needle. He swallowed, eyes watering. "Well...I, uh...I didn't. This is my first coffee today."

The twitch in the kid's smile vanished. "Well, the guy who came in first and ordered the exact same thing sure looked a hell of a lot like you."

"Same jacket? Same—"

"Same *everything*. It was *you*, man." He turned back to a pile of receipts, shaking his head.

Crazy, Daniel thought as he pushed the doors open and stepped back outside. *Totally fucking nuts.*

At least he was awake again.

THIRTY-FOUR

A ll right, Ada. I'll tell you. I'll tell you something about me. I tried to tell you once before about the country I come from. Back when we were drinking coffee, our first time out alone together. Back when I still thought there was something broken about you. Something fucked up that made you interesting. That made you beautiful.

Back when that was the only reason I wanted to get close to you.

I tried to tell you about my country, though I didn't want to slip into those stupid platitudes, those conversation crushers, where everyone gets to ooh and aah and ask dumb questions. But this is how much I liked you back then. Or at least, that's the way I liked you. Then. I tried to describe it to you. I tried, and I saw winter in your eyes. Snowscapes and dark forests. Clichéd images snatched out of stereotypes.

You stupid bitch, I thought even then. It was nothing like that.

The house I grew up in was modest, simple. That's true. A squat building, small, with mountains behind it. It was close to the railway tracks, and at night the passing trains rattled the windows and shook the doorframes. I used to have these dreams that a giant had come down over the mountains and picked our house up, gripped it in his hands, was shaking it.

I liked those dreams.

There were only two bedrooms, a small kitchen, a tiny living room, and a single bathroom I had to share with my parents. In the mornings I often stood in the passage outside by the bathroom door, my hands clasped over my crotch, dancing on the spot while my father took his time shaving or brushing his teeth, or sat on the toilet for what felt like hours reading old magazines. Or maybe just staring at the wall. I don't know.

My father, he was a handsome guy. He took care of his appearance. He put oil in his hair, he cleaned his fingernails. He was pretty neat for a railway worker. I was a little too young to know if he fucked around on my mom. It's possible, I guess. But I don't know. I doubt it somehow.

On those mornings I knew better than to knock on the door when he was in there. I held my bladder tight and danced. When the dance slowed too much, drops of urine bled into my underpants, and when my mother passed she would stop, run a hand through my hair.

"Don't hassle him," she'd say.

As if I didn't know.

Sometimes I had to abandon propriety and dash outside to pee, burning my mother's flower patch. It stung the petals and leaves so that they changed colour and curled up on themselves. I didn't like to do that—destroy my mother's things. The things she worked so hard to keep beautiful. But it was the closest place to the front door where I could safely go and not be seen. And I would never go out round the back. That was where the rabbit hutch was.

The rabbit hutch. A square shape hulking under a layer of tarp.

I had dreams about that thing, too.

Wait. I can't tell you this. What am I doing? You won't understand. You won't understand.

Will you?

THIRTY-FIVE

Ada sat slumped in her wicker chair, picking at the weave with her fingernails. She was out in her balcony studio, staring at her latest painting — or rather the canvas that was supposed to be her latest painting. The first in almost two years. Its base coat gleamed a sick, muted yellow, the colour of institution walls when someone tries to make them look "homely."

White is severity. White is empty. White is not pure or clean because the pure and clean are the most easily corrupted. One smear, one touch, one scratch. Instantly visible. Stark. I hate white. But maybe I hate yellow more.

She'd stamped on a beetle once when she was a child, and this was the exact shade that burst out between the shards of its broken shell.

Sick yellow, fucked up yellow, disgusting yellow-cream.

"It's just a base coat," she said aloud to herself. "It's just how we *start*."

She'd spent the morning cleaning her studio. Floor, worktable, desk. Every crevice, every corner. Her brushes were spotless, drying in their jar. Her various paints had been gathered and rearranged, organised by shade. She'd done this before, many times. She'd done everything except *start*. Really *start*. She sat defunct in her rag t-shirt, one of Daniel's old cast-offs, and the baggy jeans she liked to paint in. The faded fabric of the shirt was splattered with the bright stains of more productive days. Her jeans had holes worn in the pockets, the thighs streaked with stripes of colour from her habit of absently wiping her brushes off on them.

All dressed up and nowhere to go. All dolled up, and nothing to show.

She needed to paint, if not for herself then because Daniel believed she did nothing all day except lie on the couch watching TV. It was where he left her every morning, and usually where he found her every night when he came back. Daniel didn't judge her for it—*for what?*—but even so, she didn't like how it never occurred to him she might be doing something else with her day. She did plenty. She did laundry; she vacuumed; she cleaned the bathroom, polishing tiles and fastidiously removing every last stray of pubic hair Daniel shed in there. *Shed like a dog*, she sometimes thought. Last week she'd organised the fridge and gone through all the kitchen cupboards, checking expiry dates and replacing the shelf linings. She'd single-handedly hefted two heaving rubbish bags down four flights of stairs. She'd grinned like Superwoman when he came home that night, his eyes travelling her body, misreading her smile.

Still.

Damned if she'd turn into just another *housewhore*. Smug, sensible women with hips ballooning under their breezy dresses, cutting their hair short and sniffing at the younger girls. The childless girls. The girls who still looked good in knee-high boots, who were careful with their weight but not their words, who could command a room without domineering it. *As she still did, as she still was, as she still could.*

"So *do something*, bitch!" she said to herself, the snap in her tone a cruel sting, remote and alien.

This couldn't be her, speaking to her.

In the old days, when she was stuck she'd get herself a drink, sip it down in thoughtful mouthfuls as she listened to Miranda Sex Garden, Godflesh, Skinny Puppy. Something like that, depending on the mood, the moment, the atmosphere she wanted to wrap around herself. If not alcohol, then half a joint. A *blunt*, Daniel called them. A term she didn't quite understand and had never used herself. If neither of those, then she'd raid their stash, kept in an antique Oriental jewellery box she'd restored herself, touching up the chipped paint, fixing up the lacquer. A thing of beauty, oblivion locked inside.

If not alcohol or harder drugs then at least a cigarette, for God's sake. Chain-smoking while she drank cup after cup of filter coffee, thinning it with water when her hands began to shake. And painting. God...*painting*.

But all those doors were barred. Nicotine, caffeine. *Banned.* It was just her and her. Her inside of her. For now.

She sat desolate in her chair, plucking at strands of broken weave.

She missed her old life. She missed the drugs, those sweet, wild blasts of euphoria swooping through her head in a gritty line of white powder. A dizzying mouthful of smoke that veiled her world in a softly shifting haze. Daniel, for all his stalwart smiles and enthusiasm for her breakfast bran muffins, was struggling with this too. She'd noticed his exhaustion, the tremble in his fingers as he knotted his tie—like a good little office soldier—and left her every morning, a kiss on her cheek and a serviette-wrapped muffin clenched in his hand. His brow furrowed like his head ached and the Excedrin hadn't kicked in yet. This change, they hadn't planned it well enough. It had been overnight and absolute, like plunging from wild, warm waters into a still, cold pond.

Her nail snagged on the weave, and a blade punched into the bed beneath her fingernail, neat and clean, the pain sharp and sudden.

"Bitch, cunt!" she yelled, whipping her hand away. She caught the broken end of the blade and teased it out, hissing between her teeth.

She put her finger in her mouth, sucking blood. Her fingertip throbbed against her tongue. She thought of Neven, his fingers in her mouth. The thick, salty taste of his skin so much sharper than Daniel's. Tears stung behind her eyes.

Poor lost Neven, unmoored without them. Neven reduced to tedious compliments. She remembered the slow, painful way he'd put on his scarf the last time he'd come over for dinner, as though it ran an endless length and she might be tied to the end of it.

"You're not married to Neven," she said around her finger. "And Daniel didn't marry him either."

The thought made her smile. Made her wince. That magical, bestial union of three.

"But you chose this too," she told herself. "Neven was right. You could've said no."

It wasn't a new thought. Still, it made her cry.

THIRTY-SIX

The house I grew up in. It was old. It was small. I've told you that. What I haven't told you is that it was also neat. Really neat. You might appreciate how hard that is — living in the city we live in now — to maintain the beauty in beaten things, broken things. Junk. We didn't have much money, but if you walked into our house you might've been fooled into thinking we had more than we actually did. The carpets were worn but always brushed. The windows were cracked, but they shone. Every surface was polished, every shelf ordered, every cushion and pillow arranged.

That was all because of my mother. Her skills and also her obedience. My father liked to keep beauty around him. And she knew that.

"Home is where the heart is," she often said.

Okay, you'll call that *platitude.* But it meant something to her. To us.

We didn't have much on a railway worker's salary, but she did her best. Not many women can do that, find ways to create a home, to cleave comfort out of spare pennies. But she could. She did that.

The place smelled of potpourri. She made it herself with the flowers I hadn't doused in uric acid. She collected old china, buying all the mismatched and chipped pieces, the ones separated from their sets. She called them "scattered refugees of decadence." I'm translating loosely, but I think that's right. And she really was romantic like that. She bought them cheap whenever she could, and then she rearranged them—a cup that didn't fit a saucer, a bowl that didn't match a plate. She arranged them so they still looked good together. She angled them to hide their flaws. She made it work. She displayed them in an old glass cabinet that stood in the living room. That way she could see them from my dad's worn armchair. From that chair, she could see the display just right.

What I learned the most from my mother, maybe, was her talent for calm, her way of moving with quiet purpose. I loved to watch her work. I learned something about grace from her. Something about the grace of intent, I mean. When she wrote letters, peeled vegetables, folded laundry, her movements were careful and precise. She focused completely on every task, one at a time, giving each the concentration it deserved. I found that very comforting. I guess that sounds dumb. I don't expect you to understand.

Or okay, how's this? When I caught you with that needle, Ada. Did I panic? Did I? If not for my mother, I might've. Instead, I was fucking thrilled. I moved immediately into precise motion. And I know you didn't understand that. Not really. Though you didn't bother to ask. Maybe when we're through with this you'll understand. Maybe when we're done.

My father was a handsome guy. I told you that. But he was also big. Very big. And my mom, she was the smallest little thing. Petite, that's the word. He didn't talk much, seldom smoked, never drank. He had a stoic need for quiet, a love of order, an unbreakable obsession with control. In this way, I often thought my parents were perfect for each other. Where they matched, they were exactly the same. Where they were different, they met the other's absences, filling the empty spaces. Creating something whole.

It was something that, even as a kid, I dreamed of someday finding for myself.

For example. When glass was broken. When things got smashed. An hour later, you'd never know. She swept it up, she tidied it away. She never mentioned the losses again, never mourned them. There was power in that—this ability to accept, and then forget. I guess she taught me that, too.

The rabbit hutch that stood by the back door, hidden under a thick fold of green tarp, was only uncovered and opened in times when calm and control suddenly slipped. I've talked to you about how balanced everything was. Well, it wasn't that way all the time.

I've seen you slip too, Ada. In much the same way. I've seen you crack. When you're switching masks, sometimes, you've been known to fuck up. I don't want to compare you to my mother, but she was something like that too, sometimes. Maybe she was nearing her period, maybe the bills were coming in too fast. Maybe things beyond her control were reaching in, making her hands shake, making her fidget, drop things. Doubt, I guess. Doubted herself, and her ability to keep the calm in our house. A smashed cup, a stuttered word, a utensil clattering on the clean kitchen floor.

My father hated that. He'd give her a few chances. I'd see him counting them in his head. His jaw clenching. His shoulders stiffening. His eyes rolling toward her, watching her. And when she knew she was being watched, she'd get nervous. She'd be even worse. She'd fuck up again. And then again. And that was when it would all fall apart.

Her eyes would widen. She'd hold her hands up to her face. Trembling hands—what greater immediate sign of weakness is that? Already beginning to blubber, holding those hands up. Against him. Backing away.

Don't say anything. I'd think that at her. Wishing she could hear me. *Don't speak, don't cry.*

Stupid, stupid, stupid woman. I can say that about her now, in retrospect. I loved her — you know I did — but it's not like she hadn't had enough practice, or enough time to figure it out.

She knew my dad would go for her. And when he did, when he'd had enough, she'd scream.

Screaming. What a stupid fucking thing to do. You see what I mean? It invites hysteria and loss of control. It's exciting to predators. You know that.

Did you ever scream, Ada, in all the times you found yourself under that kind of threat? Did you? I don't think so. But I can't decide if that's because you're really fucking smart and know it's better to shut up, or if it's because deep down you liked it. You're shifty like that.

I've asked that question about my mother, by the way. This exact same question I have about you.

There was the rattle of the belt as it came undone, metal dancing against metal as it looped, as it swung. I remember that sound. I still dream of it sometimes. When I wake up from those dreams my dick will be hard and there'll be tears behind my eyes. Since I met you, I've thought of you in those moments in the dark. But maybe I shouldn't tell you that. I guess you don't want to know that.

Do you?

He'd grab her, drag her to the living room and bend her over the back of the armchair. Her mouth would fall open, she'd go limp, not even trying to get away as my father yanked her skirt up over her hips, tore her underwear down to her ankles. She'd grab at the plumped pillows. But she never picked them up. Never turned around. Never swung. It was like all her muscles dissolved or something. She'd lie there hanging over the back of the chair, sobbing. She stared at her display cabinet. I guess she focused on her china, the polished plates carefully arranged under glass. She had to look at something nice, maybe. In the spare seconds between each lash.

I watched all this from the doorway. I saw welts rise on her skin, wounds open. Sweat on my father's forehead. He used to grunt with each stroke, and after a while my mother would stop screaming. Too tired maybe. She'd still gasp on impact, though. And he'd keep going. Those sounds she made, you know, they're a lot like the sounds a woman makes during rough sex. Gasping for air. Gasping against the barrage of sensation. And as a guy, no matter your intentions, you never really know if its pleasure or pain that makes a woman breathe like that. When it's supposed to be consensual, sometimes you're not sure where the turn-on stops and the guilt begins. Because I'm not like Daniel. You know that.

When they both wound down, my dad would drop the belt and look at me.

"Take the tarp off the hutch," he'd say.

He kept his hand pressed to my mother's back. Holding her down. As if she'd even try to get up. To get away. She lay there collapsed over the back of the armchair, shoulders shaking, blood streaming from her ass, running down her legs. Kinda pretty, maybe. The blood, I mean.

Yes, I thought that. Even then.

I never saw her face in those moments. I have no idea what her expression was. I think sometimes it would've been good for me. If I could've seen.

But she kept her head bowed, and I obeyed my father.

I went to take off the tarp.

THIRTY-SEVEN

N even zipped through the compound gates, cresting round the curve, glancing up at Daniel and Ada's apartment windows as he passed. Ada's studio faced out this way, and he often saw her lights burning when he went by in the evenings. If he was on foot he sometimes heard the music she played while she was painting. Harsh sounds, thrashing guitars, ghostly voices bellowing, shrieking.

That girl. Maddening, crazy. Resistant, giving. Soft beneath her veneer. As all *good girls* were really, no matter how long or how well they played at being dangerous. Debauchery everlasting, it wasn't for her. He should've known months ago, long before that walk.

That goddamned walk.

There was that night a while back when some guy was talking to them, and she admitted she was married—*You? Married?*—only instead of saying, "We did it to shut our parents up," she said, "When you find the right person it's just something you want to do." That cop-out cliché sliding from her lips as Neven listened, stupefied. And then a few weeks later he suggested they give a dealer a call — it had just gone eleven and Daniel had confessed they were out of the wine — and Neven saw a look pass between husband and wife.

Ah, he'd thought. *Something's changing here.* And then pushed the thought away because it had seemed impossible to him, that Ada would walk away from him. Or rather, that she'd be able to let him walk away from her. As he had. As he wished now that he hadn't.

He was past the panic, the sense of abandonment. What he'd felt after that was a sense of loss. Replaced now by fury. But they were married, and he'd always been a third. Transient, temporary. He knew that.

What God Himself has joined…

Like God had anything to do with a couple like that.

The next time they invited him for dinner, Daniel would likely offer him a Chianti, a brandy, something sniffy and pretentious like that. One only. They'd probably end the night with a card game, Ada's vivid laughter reserved for the sly moves she made with her aces. He'd look at them both with a hunger her rich cream sauces could never satisfy. Not without the promise of that sweet, warm cream spilling from her cunt.

Neven parked the Vespa by his building, locked her up tight, looked around. He shoved his keys deep in his pockets where they wouldn't make any sound. He went round the back of the building, stepping softly on frozen ground. He stood at the gate of the old abandoned shed.

He stared into the black.

THIRTY-EIGHT

I didn't like to go anywhere near that rabbit hutch. I wouldn't touch it unless I was under orders. It was dark in there, it stank. It was cold and small inside, and there was no way to lie down or sit comfortably. When my father told me to go and take the tarp off, to unlock it, sometimes I'd go and then just stand there for a few moments, staring at it. Knowing that my mother would have to stay there all night, and maybe the next night too. I knew I would hear her sobbing and whispering to herself while I lay in bed that night, wide awake. Wishing I could go to her. Help her. If not get her out, then at least sit with her.

But my father wouldn't have let me do that.

Maybe more than anything, I obeyed because I knew what would happen when it was all over. I'd seen it many times, the beauty of the aftermath.

I did what he asked. And then I ran to my room. I didn't like to see him put her in there. Lock her up in there. Leave her there.

Later, I'd lie in bed with my pillow over my ears, comforting myself with the vision of my mother's face. Imagining how it would shine when we finally went back outside, father and son, to open the rusted padlock and let her out again. I tried not to think of her as she was then—her muscles cramping in the small confines of the cage, her stomach burning with hunger, loneliness clawing at her with nobody to hug her or kiss her or keep her company in the cold.

I told myself it didn't matter because I knew that when my father rushed back home in the afternoon, after all those hours of agonised guilt, it would be worth it. Every second of it.

Sometimes it was just a day. Sometimes it was two. My father would heat something up on the stove, slice some bread for us. But I found it hard to eat. Above all, I avoided the back door. I went out into the road during the day, walked down the winding dirt track closer to town where friends of mine might be playing. There was nothing to keep me home. No sound of her humming while she ironed, no whisper of her feet on the carpets as she walked through the house. If I got back early in the afternoons, I sat outside by the gate and waited for my father to come up over the crest of the hill. I watched for him. Sometimes he'd come back walking, a slow silhouette making its way home. And I'd know it would be a while longer. One day more.

When he did give in, it was total. Those were the only times I ever saw him run. And as soon as he was close enough, he'd yell to me, "Get to the house! Get the key!"

We kept the key in a pewter bowl on a small pine sideboard. I could never reach it fast enough. I'd be grinning, almost bursting with joy, dancing in the doorway until he caught up and snatched it out of my outstretched hand.

I let him go ahead. I followed, but I hung back. The rabbit hutch stank of her urine, her sweat. Her excrement, smeared against her thighs. Filthy things that revolted me. I didn't like to see her like that. She was like a wild animal. Like something barely human. But my father, I don't know.

Somehow I think it only made him love her more. From the way he looked at her, I got that idea. I'd stand to the side as he crouched down, as he breathed, his hands trembling, fighting with the old lock.

"Magda," he'd say softly, over and over again. "Magda, please. Please, Magda. Please."

My father was a monster, locking her up like that. I know. But even monsters can love.

Their fingers met through the bars, the hatch came open, and with tears running down his cheeks, he'd lift her up and pull her into his arms.

Ada. Imagine that. The beauty of it.

It didn't matter how dirty she was, how messed up she was, how bad she smelled. He loved her. He loved her, and he was sorry, and in her moment of gratitude, I saw in her face that she never loved him more than she did then. When he went back for her. When he released her.

This is what I learned that you and Daniel only skirted around the edges of. The beauty of chaos, of violence. How it breaks and then it binds. A bond tighter than any other.

After, it was my job to clean out the rabbit hutch. I had to wrestle the layer of soiled fabric out from the bottom and wash it under the tap. Scrubbing it until it bore only stains, trace smells. I cleared the cage of cobwebs and used pliers to straighten the bends my mother had made in the bars. Then I covered it with the tarp.

At night, I'd listen to them having sex. Making love, maybe. Gentler, slower than at other times. I never looked in on them. I never watched. But I knew somehow the expressions they would have on their faces. Ecstasy and adoration.

I know he held her close.

THIRTY-NINE

The next sighting was of Ada, and Daniel was the one who saw it.

Walking the two blocks from his office to the subway station, a thin crowd pushing around him, too many voices too close to his ear. Bodies and hair and musty clothes. A few drifts of perfume sliding between the sour smells of sweat and oil and dirty skin. The astounding filth of this city. He thought of home, clean carpets and polished tile, the sweet, smoky tones of incense caught in the curtains.

One day they would move to the suburbs. Sign a ten-year lease on one of those fixer-uppers by the river, let Ada paint whatever walls she liked however she damn well wanted. They'd need a car of course, but there was enough time and money for that. The important thing was that these ideas were not as impossible now as they had seemed just six months ago.

We'll have a baby on the way by then, he thought.

The hassle of the crowd forgotten, he ran down the steps and into the station with a smile of wonder.

He'd just pushed through the turnstiles when he saw her. She was ahead of him, going down the steps that led to the platform. Her hair was clipped up in a messy twist, the way she did it when she showered in the mornings without washing it, damp strands drying in soft curls. She was wearing her red leather jacket, the one with the belt he knew was fraying at the buckle. She was stepping fast down the stairs, her head bowed, watching her feet. The back of her neck a soft curve, smooth skin bare of a scarf.

She'll get sick.

This was his first thought. The one that struck him before he wondered what she was doing there.

"Ada!"

He hurried to the top of the stairs, just glimpsing her as she hit the platform and strode on ahead, a flash of auburn hair in the clusters and drifts of people that moved, stood, loitered, some dragging bags, some turning their heads. Groups of out-of-towners stopping short to read the information boards on the pillars on either side, oblivious to the bottlenecks swelling behind them.

It was futile to call out to her. Not across this distance, not in this crowd. He knew she would be heading to the far end of the platform, to the carriages right at the back where she'd be more likely to get a seat. She was moving fast, because the trains were only three minutes apart and she would hate to stay here in this station a second longer than she had to. She'd want to get on the very next train, doors sealing her in, announcements blaring, taking her away from the city's hectic, tumultuous outer circle. *And on to where?*

He reached the bottom of the stairs and glimpsed her far ahead. A woman dragging a suitcase had just cut across her path, almost tripping her. Ada's hands flew out of her pockets to grab at balance. She side-stepped, shooting a glare at the woman. Even across the distance he saw the flare in Ada's cheeks.

She wasn't a city girl. She never had been, really. She hated this chaos, this kind of crush.

So what is she doing out here, so far from home?

He ran after her, pushing past people, zigzagging to cut in front of the woman with the suitcase, making her stumble. He paused for just an instant, apologising with a malicious grin. He'd tell Ada about that later. She'd like that.

The train had pulled up; the doors were opening. She was veering left to step into the carriage. He angled through the crowd, rushing after her. It didn't occur to him to jump onto the train at the nearest door and then travel down as it moved, searching until he found her. He was too fixed on that slim figure in a red jacket, that messy twist of hair, that woman, *his wife*, found in a crowd and oblivious to him.

The warning beeps sounded as he neared her carriage door, the doors sliding into action just as he was about to step on. His heart lurched, thundered in his throat as the doors clicked home. He stepped back, beaten. He returned his hands to their familiar clutch, deep in his coat pockets. Clenching. The crowd, momentarily quelled, surged back around him. Looking up as the train began to move, he saw her just beyond the doors. She was standing square in front of him, her jacket belted, the V where it crossed at her chest pulled wide enough to reveal the black lace of her bra, enough to show that not only was she bare of a scarf but of a shirt, too.

She did that once at Red House, he just had time to remember before he met her eyes. *That drunk guy grabbed at her when he fell over and ripped her shirt right off. She belted her jacket over her bra and laughed, said she was going for the dominatrix look.*

This memory just had time to travel his mind in its entirety, and then his eyes met hers through the glass. And his heart, still thundering, gave an awkward jab. Sharp enough to hurt.

She was looking directly at him. There was no surprise in her face, no humour, no love. Pure hatred spat from her eyes, raw and ripe, a power of malign loathing thick enough to stop his breath, enough to wash him in a wave of nauseous vertigo.

She sees me.

The train gained speed and whipped away, screaming down the dark tunnels.

FORTY

Do you understand me, Ada? Are you listening yet? You're shivering. Are you that cold? Why did you stop trying to talk? I need to know you're still here with me, listening to me. Ada, look at me. Please.

FORTY-ONE

Neven lay on his bed, his hands laced behind his head. Gripping clumps of hair between his fingers, tugging as he eased his hands apart, relaxed. Away, and back. He liked the sensation of his skin tightening, a line of pain zipping down the back of his head. The idea that if he yanked hard enough he might split it, peel the sheath of skin that covered his skull right off. Curl it down over his eyes, rip again at his nostrils to free that cartilage hook. Reveal his true face.

Of course, it didn't work like that. That was horror movie fantasy, unreal against the true mechanics of the body, the knit and weave of fat and flesh, nerves and muscles wired tight beneath.

No, it's not possible like that. I know. I'm just having thoughts.

And thoughts were maybe all he had left. He knew that, too.

He thought of the old bicycle shed. Three walls of cracked concrete, a sheet of chain-link fencing curled over its black mouth, secured, run red with rust. The ground around it a wild nest of weeds and brambles, dry twigs stung with cold, snapping against the icy earth where he stepped. It was a disused space, discarded.

As he was disused, discarded.

In the summer, folks in the compound took their dogs out there to shit, to run in circles, enfeebled mixed-breeds excited by the sudden pseudo-wildness of their surroundings, reminding them of the time when they were wolves. To be ravenous, powerful, free. That was in the summer, but not now in the dead of cold. Now the only sounds coming from there were the yowls and ethereal shrieks of stray cats as they fought, as they mated. Disconcerting, until you put your pillow over your head, or switched on the TV, or turned the music up.

This is what happens in cities, where you pile hundreds of people on top of each other in close quarters. Everyone becomes immune to the sounds of screaming.

He sat up on his elbows, dizzy at the surge of blood pulsing around his skull. He sat up, almost expecting it when his phone on the bedside table buzzed a message. It was from Daniel: SPEAK TO ADA TODAY?

He frowned, typed his reply: NO WHY?

He waited for a few minutes to see if Daniel would answer. When he didn't, Neven slid his legs over the edge of the bed to stand. He walked to the kitchen, the cold floor numbing the soles of his feet, each step gathering grime. Unlike Ada and Daniel, playing house had never interested him. He didn't care about the marks on the walls or the mould in the bathroom. Hell, it didn't even bother him that he had to boil his water in a pot on the stove, since he'd never got round to buying a kettle and doubted he ever would. Visiting Daniel and Ada was always a little surreal. *Welcome to Adultland!* Coffee sets and special hand soap, fresh tablecloths and vacuumed rugs. They'd never been up to his apartment. Which struck him in that moment as odd that it had never happened, not once in the time he'd been close to them. In the beginning he wouldn't have minded, but now if they did come by he'd be ashamed for them to see it. So pitifully desolate. A functional set of stark white walls. The landlord's crummy furniture, mismatched and mostly broken, trailed throughout the rooms. It made a statement, this place. *I am lonely. And I am alone.*

If Ada — or Daniel, but especially Ada — were to see how he lived, it would only make them feel smug about their new lifestyle. Justified. That they had risen above this and on into maturity, responsibility. Savings plans and insurance payments. Decent sleeping hours and healthy eating habits. No more living like footloose twenty-somethings, erratic and disbelieving, choking on those first frantic breaths of adult freedom.

No more drugs.

No more getting drunk.

No more crazy sex with their best friend.

He stood frozen in front of the fridge for a vacant moment, then yanked the door open and took the last of his beers. He'd need to go downstairs to stock up. Maybe he'd even grab a bottle of cheap vodka. Back home he'd stick some music on and drink it in the dark, waiting for the shadows and echoes in his head to build, to close in.

He'd see how far they took him.

FORTY-TWO

Ada. Before you and Daniel broke off from me, we had that time. Just you and me. That final time alone.

I remember that day. You lay beside me, bare, your head turned away from me, your hair scattered across Daniel's pillow in soft curls. The colour changed in the semi-darkness, from auburn to dark brown. You drew the curtains before we undressed, changing the light. Was that for vanity, or paranoia that somehow we were being watched? I wasn't sure. I didn't ask.

You lay on Daniel's side and I lay on yours because you didn't want me in his territory. As though that could in any way minimise the betrayal of you and me alone in your apartment like that. The close space on the insides of your thighs still glistening, a used condom dropped on the floor beside me like a strangled slug. And I had this sensation of movement on each side of my waist, my nerves still tingling from the silky chafe of your thighs. Because you liked to wrap your legs right around me, and the faster I moved, the more I felt it. And kept on feeling it. I love how you did that.

"We didn't make love," you said. "There's no such thing."

"We fucked, then?" I asked you.

You laughed. "No. Sex. Just sex. Let's just call it that."

"All right then."

We used a generic term with no complications, no connotations. But it was still you and me alone on Daniel's bed. No blades, no blood, no drugs. Just the smell of sweat and rubber and secretions. Your wedding ring on the table beside you. The fact of that ring annoyed me — its existence — and though I knew I had no right, I didn't care that it bothered me. He'd given you that shining thing you had to remove before you would touch me. Licking your finger first to help it slide off. I had to fight to forget about it because I wanted to be with you, savour the minutes I had alone with you.

Even sated, the energy between us hummed. My dick, aching, lay curled against my thigh in a confused, exhausted state. Semi-turgid, not quite resting. I ran my hands all over your body. I wanted to know I'd touched you everywhere, the smooth undersides of your arms, the space between your shoulder blades. The sides of your neck, every angle of your thighs. Your wrists, your knees, the groove of your spine.

You turned onto your back. You angled your legs away from me, and your hip rose. My hand followed the slopes. Your belly. Your breasts. Your scar.

"Tell me how you got this."

You flinched. "Got what?"

"This scar. This."

"Oh. That." Your tone was stiff, dismissive. But I think you were pretending, feigning boredom while your mind raced. "I did that."

"No you didn't."

You turned to face me, your eyebrow raised. "Yes. I did." Emphatic. "I did it when I was twenty-four. About a year before I came here."

That scar, it followed the curve beneath your left breast and worked its way up, stopping just below the point where your cleavage met when you wore a tight bra.

"How?" I asked you. "Why?"

You laughed—laughed?—and shook your head. "You wouldn't understand."

"Yes," I said. "Yes, I would. I think I would. Tell me."

"I wanted to cut my breast off."

"Why?"

You sighed, an irritated rattle of breath. "Because I thought if I did that I would have to be honest with myself. And other people would have to be honest with me, too. Because when you're mutilated, people don't want to look at your body. They have to see your soul. That was the theory, at least."

"But you didn't. I mean, you didn't...cut it off."

"No. I tried, and I was serious about trying, but it hurt too much."

"But, Ada..."

I touched that curve. It followed the contours of your breast so exactly. An intense, ragged roadway of thickened tissue. Stopping abruptly at a point that spun in a starburst of scars.

"You gored yourself here," I said, recognising what it had to—could only—have been. A blade twirled. Ripping on all sides. Making a hole.

"At the last minute, I thought I'd try to stab myself in the heart instead."

"But you didn't."

"No. I told you. I could barely handle getting through soft tissue, how could I cut through muscle, get past bone? It hurt too much."

I bent to kiss it. The whole of it. I followed its length with my tongue. Your skin was salty because I'd made you sweat. Your heart was beating staccato because I'd made you talk. Made you tell me this. Made you remember. You let me do it, kiss you like that. You didn't flinch that time.

"You need to go now," you said when I raised my head. "I only invited you over today because it was time to change the sheets anyway. And Daniel will be home in an hour or two."

"Now?"

"Yes. Now. I still have to run the machine."

You lay stiff on the bed, your hair dark in the light, your curves and angles obscure in the shadows. For a moment, you looked a little different. For a moment, I wondered if it was really you.

I put my clothes on. You didn't move. "I'm going now."

I waited. But you didn't say goodbye.

FORTY-THREE

S he'd started the painting. She'd made the initial strokes, the ones that slide off the brush in clumsy strikes, awkward and hard-edged without shading, without context. Free-form painting was a test of commitment, also of memory. That first precious glimpse of the concept flitting through the remote edges of her brain, a cobweb strung between quivering branches. Look at it one minute and it was clear and real, and her passion for it surged. Look at it again, and it shifted to obscurity. Futile, ridiculous. Too vague, too wishful.

Impossible. Sometimes it seems.

But for now she felt good. She stood in the shower with her eyes closed, her fingers clawing soap out of her hair, her head tilted back. The spray hit her forehead in a constant, numbing fall.

It's going to be okay. It is. It will.

She wasn't sure what time Daniel would be home. Soon, she hoped. After her shower, she'd put on one of those roomy, cosy floor dresses she'd bought in Cambodia. She'd put on a hint of lipstick, a stroke or two of mascara. Dinner was a casserole she'd thrown together, and it was ready to go in the oven at a moment's notice. There was a case of Lite beer in the fridge for him, soda water and grape juice for her. She wouldn't ask him for a sip. She'd smile at him and kiss him and keep her hands from twisting in her lap.

Just because things are changing doesn't mean I'm no longer me, she'd assured him, herself, again and again.

That had to be true, especially now that it was too late to turn back.

She slid her hands down past her breasts and paused at her abdomen, pressing. A protective V, thumb to thumb, palms to skin, hot water shushing around her, over her in a smooth, warm pulse.

FORTY-FOUR

It doesn't help to think of the good times. Good times? I want to talk about the dark times. Insanity, depravity. Even now I look back on it, this journey that we shared not so long ago, and I can't believe the things we did. The things that happened. That we made happen. The three of us. Not those other times, when it was just you and me alone. Because it's like we were different people then. Like we weren't who we are. Or maybe we were who we are? Which versions are real? I don't know the difference myself just yet. I only know that at some point, yes, something split.

You want to talk about cutting. You want to talk about wounds. You want to talk about Daniel fucking a hole he put in some girl's breast. You want to talk about it like you're a victim too, like you and I had nothing to do with it. But I felt you. How wet you were. You were fucking me at the time, remember? Sitting on my lap. And I know you liked it, watching Daniel gore that hole. I know. I felt you. I was there.

You want to talk about damage. Maybe the first time away from Daniel was a kind of rape. Maybe. But you want to talk to me about these things like you hate me, when we both know that isn't true. Or if it is, it's neatly entwined with hatred's twin. Siamese style, grotesque. Honest.

Because I'm pretty sure you love me.

Still. None of that matters. Drugging strangers and marking them up was Daniel's thing. He liked cutting you; he liked cutting me. You let him fuck up that beautiful tattoo of yours with his little razor blades, his heated needles. I've got scars of my own from him, in case you forget. The one on the back of my neck. I can't see it, of course, but I feel it with the tips of my fingers. A small line where the skin is a little thinner, where the scar healed too wide.

I touch it sometimes when I want to remember that night.

That night. You lay back on the couch and lifted your skirt, but it was Daniel who stripped you. Opened your legs. He raised his eyebrow at me with that drunken leer. That madman-shocked-sane expression he sometimes has. His hair was wild. He looked ridiculous.

"Ours, yes?" he asked.

"A scar should have a good story." You slurred that at me, your eyelids heavy. Lying complicit with a bellyful of Campari and a straight-razor in your hand. For a moment I thought you wanted to slit my throat. I was never really sure with you on those nights. But then Daniel stepped away and you called me over. I stood over you, staring down at you. Knowing I would fall. High on coke, which I still wasn't really used to. Stripping off my clothes. Collapsing onto you. Kissing you. You tasted bitter from the drugs, sweet from the Campari. You pulled back and closed your mouth on my chin, catching my stubble against your teeth. Letting me breathe. Knowing I needed to breathe.

I found my way between your legs. You crossed your legs behind my back. A total embrace. I felt like I was out of my own body, out of my own mind. And while part of me stayed present with you, some other parts of me were falling into something else. Fucking you was always like that. Like being in two worlds at once.

I didn't see you pass the razor to Daniel. But I knew something was up when you closed your arms around my back. So tight. Too tight. Planning to — wanting to — hold me in place. As if you'd have the strength. You arched up against me, pressing your breasts tighter to my chest. Trying to distract me.

You said in my ear, "Shhh."

You strengthened your grip. I think you locked your hands behind me. And then I felt the blade's edge at the nape of my neck. Pressing, biting. I almost thrashed. For an instant I wanted to fight free, but I knew what that thing was. The damage it could do if I moved.

And I did it for you. I let it happen. For you.

I hissed through my teeth when he cut me. A long, slow slide of pain, the blade sinking past my skin.

A man's mouth is rough on wounds. I preferred the smooth brush of your cheeks, your chin, your tongue moving across my skin in careful licks.

"Relax," you said. "Find that place in yourself. Just enjoy it."

You were high, you were drunk. But we all were. Later, when my blood had stopped, we went to the bedroom and you lay between us. Daniel rolled you onto your belly. He cut you, too. You shrieked in pain, in laughter. Mutilating the image you had sold your body to have inked into your flesh.

Don't say you didn't like it. I saw your face. I was there too. I kissed the blood off your skin just the same as Daniel did. I know your taste. I still taste you. Metallic, sweet.

When we were done with you, you skipped to the bathroom with your hands covering your breasts. Prudish, ecstatic as a tween caught topless in a lake. The lines of blood, smeared and dried, added new dimensions to your tattoo.

Maybe I understood then why Daniel hated that swan so much.

"All the great love stories involve at least a little blood," Daniel said to me while you were gone. Rolling back, satisfied. The pretentious fuck.

The thing is, Ada, I've had a lot of girls in my life. Sometimes they wanted me and sometimes they didn't. Sometimes they bit and scratched like you bit, like you scratched. Sometimes I made them bleed and sometimes they got blood from me. But this intimacy we had, the two of us—no, the three of us—I never knew anything like it. And I know you felt it, too.

But more than that, more than any of that, remember this, Ada: you came to me.

FORTY-FIVE

Where did you go today?"

"Nowhere."

"I saw you at the subway station. What were you doing there?"

"I wasn't there. I was here all day. I didn't leave."

"I saw you."

"It wasn't me."

"Yes it was." Pacing, fidgeting. "I saw you." Clawing his hands through his hair. "It was you. Why are you lying to me? I saw you. It was *you*."

FORTY-SIX

For the third night in a row, Neven woke on the floor beside his bed, face pressed against the soiled tile, hands dead under the weight of his hips. Numb fingers groping at his crotch.

He heard her voice in echo. *You poor thing.*

Behind him, above him. Or from somewhere in his head. Ada had said this to him once when she woke him on her and Daniel's living room floor. He'd been lying in a pose much like this, and she said it mocking, teasing, stooping to help lift him to his feet.

You poor thing.

Helping him up because he was too drunk or too high or too much of both and she was playing mommy. Playing like she cared about him, this thing she and Daniel bled.

Now he freed his hands and grabbed the edge of the bed, pulling himself up. The shades weren't drawn and the city skyline hovered beyond the glass. Square blocks solid against the smog, a few lights glowing in the pre-dawn darkness. Night owls, or discrete sleepers who preferred to dream in daylight. Or insomniacs pacing empty rooms.

Ada grew up in the country, in a place far from here. He remembered her telling him once that it still surprised her, how a city crammed with so many people actually slept. Empty streets and silent buildings. The stillness of night astonished her.

He walked to the window, his steps dragging, his hands prickling as blood returned and nerves woke. Like ants biting just beneath the skin. His head throbbed. His tongue felt like it had been wrapped in a strip of old tape, soiled with fluff, held thick in his mouth. He pressed his forehead against the window and gazed down. From where he stood he could just make out the edge of the shed far below. The roof sheathed with a fresh layer of ice, the ragged ends of tangled trash flicking around in the low breeze. He tapped the window with a burning finger. Steady beats. He stayed like that, fixed in place, until the moon had vanished, a glow kissed the sky and the cold glass had turned his forehead numb.

FORTY-SEVEN

Ada, are you cold enough?
Ada, are you feeling yet?
Ada, wake up.

FORTY-EIGHT

The next time it happened, she saw them.

Painting in the calm of her studio, no music, her heartbeat whispering in her ears as her brushes swept colour, swirled water. Her palette knife cutting into jars of paint, scooping it out like gaudy pudding. Blues and greens, hints of grey and earthy browns.

She was too focused at first to notice the buzzing in her head. It rose in a sharp, frantic hum, like a chainsaw somewhere in the distance, screaming through hard wood. Screaming through metal. Screaming at her.

She put her brush down and wiped her hands off on her jeans, adding to the wet mix of watery colours she collected there. She shook her head. The sound wasn't coming from the outside. It came from inside of her. Or if it came from the outside, it wasn't a sound with physical cause, rather it was something beamed in. A vibration matched to some hidden resonance only she could hear. It crept through her like a nest of ants pouring up her brain stem and spilling out into her skull. Trampling neural pathways, burning, biting.

She raised her hands and gripped the sides of her head. Her hair knotted between her fingers. She pulled. A zip-line of pain formed where her scalp stretched. Real pain, at least. Something she could fully feel. She stood and walked to the windows, looking down on the road that ran through the compound. And she saw them.

Neven and Daniel were out there, alone in the early afternoon hush with their faces turned up to her window. They were both stamping their feet, waving their arms. Their faces a hectic red, their mouths moving in fury. Madmen ranting and raving at her. Instead of words, the buzzing rose, cracking through her skull in an explosion of heat. Not ants. Lava. So much fire and pain her breaths stopped in her chest and swelled there, aching in her lungs. She stumbled back from the windows, her hands still pulling at her hair. She fell against the sliding doors and sat down hard, her legs lashing out as she kicked at air, as if kicking them away.

Her painting, her self-portrait, half-finished but fully formed, watched. Black eyed, green-faced, its teeth a sharp and perfect white, a razor-blade smile set at jagged angles.

FORTY-NINE

I want to make an appointment. I want an abortion. As soon as possible please. Please."

"Honey, maybe you should sit down."

"When's the soonest I can do it? Please."

"Sit down, Miss…uh…Anna, right?"

"Ada. My name's Ada. How do you know me?"

"Ada, take a seat okay? Would you like to talk to someone? I can find a counsellor for you. Just…sit for a minute. I'll bring you some water."

"I don't need water. I need an abortion, and I need one now. As soon as you can or I'll do it myself."

"Honey, you already had your abortion, remember? You came in just last week. It went…fine. You're fine."

* * *

On the way back home from the clinic, she saw herself. Coming down the pavement in her direction, her head lowered, stepping fast. She was wearing the red jacket she'd thrown out in the autumn, after the strap with the buckle came off. The jacket she'd loved, that Daniel had loved. Calling her a dominatrix when she wore it with a low-cut shirt and a push-up bra. A look Neven loved too, pressing his face between her breasts, his arms closed around her, palms pressed to her back. Roving.

It's wrong, she remembered thinking, even in bliss. Knowing even then that she could never admit this doubt to Daniel, or to him.

All these memories and impressions stumbled through her when she saw herself out there on the street, marching down the pavement toward her. *Jacket, belt, dominatrix, Neven, his face, my chest, wrong. It's wrong!*

Her other her was about to look up. She knew her own gestures. The hand coming out the pocket to sweep back her hair, a self-conscious movement she made before she looked around because in the back of her mind she was always afraid that someone was watching her, studying her.

It's me. I'm watching. It's me that's been watching me.

But this was her not as she was now, in her red sash dress and tan boots, her clunky big day bag thrown over her shoulder. This was her as she'd been six months ago—thinner, sharp-chinned, scarlet lipstick, messy hair and too much eyeliner. Panda eyes, like she'd been crying.

Because she'd cried a lot back then.

Don't look up. Don't look at me. Don't—

But she did.

The ground rippled, vertigo overtaking. For a moment she almost swooned. She put her hands over her head, ready to scream. Those black eyes stared back at her in shock, in surprise. The her that couldn't be her was wearing eye shadow, disco blue. It sparkled in the light.

My God. It's real. She's real. I'm really real—

But instead of screaming, words clambered up her throat in frenzy and heat and fury. "You whore. You fucking whore. Stay away from me, you whore!"

Startled pedestrians looked at her in alarm, their expressions switching from fright to concern at the hot tears rushing down her cheeks. She clutched her bag to her chest like it might protect her, something instinctive telling her to cover her heart. Her arms crossed over it, she sucked in lungfuls of icy, leather-scented air.

She turned and ran. Desperate to widen the gap, to put distance between herself and this other her, this her that couldn't be, believing the wider the space between them, the easier it would be to tell herself, *It wasn't you. She wasn't real. You're pregnant and it's making you crazy, but she's the one who killed the baby and she's not real. It'll pass. It'll pass because it has to and everything is okay. Everything will be okay.*

FIFTY

But you're not really her.
You're not really here.

FIFTY-ONE

Daniel found the note before he saw the painting. It was sitting on the coffee table, scrawled on the back of a receipt.

I'm leaving. Don't follow me.
Ada

A buzzing filled his head in the place where his thoughts used to be. His heart surged and thundered in his chest, his knees begged to buckle, but he stood very stiff and very straight, the note trembling in his hand.

Was it rage he felt, under the hiss of his heart? Shock? Disbelief? Beneath the stillness that swept through him, whatever it was seemed apart from him. Other. Excised.

She was pregnant, of course. He didn't know how he knew that, but he did. They'd planned their baby and changed their lives to make room for it, and now that it was on its way, she was leaving him. A part of him almost understood, or might later. Once the rage had made itself known, claimed him, then moved on. If it would. If it could.

Walking through the rooms, he saw her scarves and jackets were gone from the stand, her shoes from the rack. She hadn't taken everything of hers, but she'd taken most of it. Her wardrobe almost bare, her underwear drawers swept clean. The only sign of hurry was out in her studio. Those crummy old jeans she wore when she painted lay on the floor like she'd just stepped out of them. The crotch open between the circles left by the shape of her legs. As though she'd vanished where she stood. Her brushes and paints were strewn around in disarray, the jar of water still full, the colour muddy green like scum in pond water.

He walked around to look at the painting on her easel. He saw green, black, red. The face blurred in front of his eyes, then slowly came clear.

We should've known we weren't supposed to change, he thought, staring at it. *Not a couple like us. Or maybe it's that we should never have been.*

The portrait was of Ada, of course. He'd know her face anywhere, even in abstract, even when mutilated like this. A monstrous thing with hellish eyes, features a stippled series of furious jabs. Green paint, red paint, grey. Like moss growing on skin. A monster. The evil in its expression clawed through every brushstroke, locked itself in every line.

For a moment he stopped breathing. The Ada in the painting stared back, somehow gleeful, somehow indifferent.

"Get out of here, Ada," he breathed. The words came without thought in his sudden terror, giving her permission she'd never hear. "Go."

His phone rang. For a moment he thought it might be Ada, but it couldn't be. No. She wouldn't call. Would she?

He looked at the screen.

It was Neven.

Thank you, he thought when he saw the name, a wave of rich gratitude momentarily stunning him. Friends. At least he had a friend. One who knew more than any other, one who would understand everything. *Thank you, Neven. You couldn't have timed this better.*

He answered the call.

FIFTY-TWO

N even didn't greet him. His first words to Daniel were, "I've got her."

I've got her.

Don't worry. She came to me.

Come.

FIFTY-THREE

You came to me.

You met me outside my building and I took you upstairs. I was worried about the dirt, the mess, the state of the place, but you didn't look at anything around you. As soon as I'd closed the door you took off your coat, pulled off your boots. Then you took your shirt off and the thermal vest underneath. For a moment I thought you wanted sex, thought maybe you'd been missing me and wanted one last time with me, you and me together alone, a frenzy of sweat. A desperate goodbye. But you stood back, and you faced me in your bra, your jeans. Your breasts swelled with every inward breath, fast and tight, and I saw it then, the adrenaline rushing through you. I almost heard it. Your heartbeat. I saw the pulse in your neck, the thin sheen of sweat on your forehead. Your pupils were pinpoints in brilliant blue.

"I don't want it," you said. "I don't know if I still have it but I know I don't want it. They won't help me, but you will. You can do this for me, Neven. I trust you to. I trust you. I do."

I had an idea of what you meant, but I needed you to say it. I stepped away from you, folded my arms. I sniffed. I tried to look nonchalant, bored. Annoyed. You always responded when I cut you off, when I shut you down. Something inside of you softened when I reacted like that. And it worked. Your eyes shone, then reddened. A thin film of tears appeared. You blinked and those tears rushed down your cheeks, pure and perfect. I wanted to step forward and kiss them off your cheeks. I wanted to put my arms around you. I had to be careful not to smile.

I never thought I'd feel such joy, seeing you cry.

"Please," you said.

"But I don't know what you're talking about, Ada. You sound pretty crazy to me. And you look it too, by the way. Are you on anything?"

"Jesus Christ, Neven!" You buckled, you burst. You leant your hands on your knees and you ducked your head, breathing hard to fight away your tears. Your slim, pale shoulders shuddered. "I might be pregnant," you said to the floor. "I don't know. There's this woman, this other me. She did something, I don't know what. Or maybe I did something. I don't remember. I don't know. I'm not high. But I think I'm going crazy. And I can't have a baby. Not this. Not this…thing."

Your hair had slipped over your shoulders, obscuring your face. I'd never seen such chaos in you. This wildness caught in you. It made you beautiful, your colour vivid, energy crackling across your skin. As if a truer shade of you was finally breaking free. You looked up at me, tossed your hair out of your face. You breathed.

"Punch me," you said. "Right here." You pressed a hand over the soft stretch of your pelvis. The tender, boneless expanse between your hips.

I shrugged. "All right. But take your clothes off first."

You stopped.

"I mean it. At best they're gonna be in the way, at worst you're gonna mess them up. Take them off."

You stared at me, stupefied. I saw you thinking. Then you nodded. I leaned back against the wall and watched you undress, my arms folded, slowly chewing my lower lip. Bra, jeans, tights, panties. Off. Your bare skin was smooth as milk in the light.

You stood delicately, with your feet crossed, as if you didn't want me to look between your legs. At that place I already knew so well. "It's cold in here," you said, rubbing your arms.

"No it's not." I took my jacket off, pausing to throw it toward the kitchen table. I missed, and it landed on the floor with a heavy *thump.* I stepped toward you.

"Wait!" You held up your hand. "Listen to me. Don't mess around. You need to punch me hard. Really hard. Do it as hard as you want. As hard as you can. I know you can hurt me. I want you to hurt me. No, I don't want you to hurt me—"

You stopped, breathing hard. I saw it in your eyes, the speed of your thoughts. Flashing by like liquid fire.

"I want you to kill it. Hit me hard enough to kill it. If it's there."

"Wait a minute," I glowered at you. "You want me to kill your baby? You want me to kill a fucking baby?" I asked this just to see the crestfallen look on your face. To see your desperation build. Because it was beautiful. You were so beautiful, broken like this.

"Goddammit!" You began crying again. "I want you to punch me! That's what I want."

"Say it."

"Say what?"

"Tell me you want me to hurt you. Tell me how much you want me to hurt you. Tell me that's the reason why. Not some bullshit about some baby."

For a moment I thought you might smile. There was a glimmer of light in your face, a flash of happiness. The briefest.

Then gone. But I knew it had been there. I'd seen that look before.

"I want you to fuck me up." You kept your eyes fixed on mine. "I want you to fuck me up. Like I want you to fuck me."

I almost smiled myself. "Tell me again. Tell me more."

"I want you to hurt me like you love me like you hate me. I want you to make me bleed. I want you to fuck me in the ass with a knife up my cunt—double-edged, cold—adding slits to my slits and putting holes in my holes. Sweetness and blood for you to feel, to taste. And even if you spit it out, the taste of me will stay. I want—"

Obscene, this shit you were saying. You were still talking when I stepped toward you, into your space. You weren't expecting it, lost in your dream, your eyes glazed over. Still talking. I clenched my fist. I punched you full force, pulling all the strength through my shoulder and down my arm. Into my hand. Into the soft of your belly.

There was a thick, meaty whack. And you flew. You collapsed against the wall, gasping, your eyes rolling back. You slid to the floor like a rag doll. Helpless, void of strength. Tears shimmered down your cheeks.

"Breathe," I told you.

And you obeyed me. You fought for air, tearing it down into your lungs in tight, frantic gasps that lengthened into drawn, desperate choking sounds. I waited until your breaths evened out. I was still wearing my boots. You looked up at just that instant, as I stepped forward, and your eyes widened. You barely had time to say it—No—before I came at you again. This time I kicked you, the toe of my boot vanishing in your abdomen. A little too high. I heard a low cracking sound, like a twig wrapped in a wet towel, snapped. All the colour vanished from your face and your mouth opened. You gaped. You were probably trying to scream but didn't have the air for it.

I bent down beside you and put my hand between your legs. I pressed, slipped my fingers inside. There was a tremor in your thighs, like for a moment you tried to squeeze your legs together. Like you wanted to stop me but didn't have the strength.

"You're wet." I withdrew my hand. I inspected it. "But that's not blood."

I sucked the taste of you off the tips of my fingers. You were breathing fast and your skin shone with a fresh burst of sweat. Pain. I knew the look. It consumed you. An intense blankness filled your wide-open eyes, as if you were struck staring at something I couldn't see. Something beyond me, something beyond you. Revealed. I watched your face, fascinated.

"It hurts? Relax. Find that place inside yourself. Enjoy it."

I settled down beside you. I lifted your head into my lap. After a minute or two you fell asleep, or passed out, I don't know. A trace of saliva leaked past your lips. It might've been the light, but for a moment I thought the colour was a little electric. Maybe a little pink.

FIFTY-FOUR

I've got her."

"What do you mean, you've got her? Who's *her*?"

"Ada, of course. I've got her. She came to me. Come round the back of my building tonight. There's an old bicycle shed there. I'll show you. She can't leave. We won't let her leave. Not until we fetch the key. Not until she's ready."

"What the fuck are you talking about? She's gone. She's probably at the airport already, about to get on a plane to —"

"No she's not. She doesn't have any money, remember? Or if she did, not enough. Where could she go? Who else would she go to?"

"Neven —"

"Just come by. It'll be... Daniel, it'll be wonderful. You'll see."

FIFTY-FIVE

T hey met at the side of the building. Neven waited for him just out of the circle of light cast by the last lamppost, leaning against the wall with his arms folded tight against the thick padding of his jacket. He breathed dense streams of condensation into the night winter cold. His hood was up, his head down. He stood tense, frozen, holding himself in. A statue cast black, free of light. When he saw Daniel approaching, he straightened up and went to him.

They embraced in the darkness.

"Is it *her*, Neven? Is it actually *her*?"

"Yeah. Come on."

Their boots squeaked through the fine layer of fresh snow, the new fall still drifting over their heads. Thickening. Neven rummaged through his pockets and brought out a set of keys, still shiny, gleaming, unblemished. Padlock keys. Daniel knew by the shape. They made their way off the footpath and up into the small section of empty land between the back of the building and the perimeter wall.

The narrow concrete shed waited in winter quiet. The snow on its roof was lit with a low amber glow, cast by the few scattered lights still shining out from the windows above. Lights left on by night owls, or discrete sleepers who preferred to dream in daylight. Insomniacs pacing empty rooms. Secret lives. Unseen eyes moving around the apartments, their locked compartments, slippered feet shushing on grimy tile. It gave Daniel the sense that perhaps he and Neven were being watched.

But of course, in a city like this, everybody watches. Everybody looks. And nobody sees a thing.

The mouth of the shed was closed off with a sheet of chain-link. The space beyond it was vacuous, lightless. The gate, a steel frame netted with chain, was invisible from a distance, camouflaged against the fencing. With no light inside the shed, it was impossible to see beyond it.

"What is this place?" Daniel asked, surveying it.

"Nothing anymore," said Neven. "Nobody knows about it."

Stillness descended. Snowflakes the size of pennies joined. Soft as paper. The kiss of ice. Daniel brushed it off his nose. "It's fucking cold," he said.

"It's not so bad." Neven slid the key into the padlock and unhooked it. He yanked at the gate and it came free with an icy crack, swinging open with a brief metallic scream.

A sound came from within the black. Something that was almost words, the whisper of a moan.

Ada?

Daniel's heart surged, skipped into frenzy. "That's her? She's in there?"

Neven stood aside for him. "Quick."

They slipped inside. Neven swung the gate shut behind him. "I set a gas lantern down here somewhere."

Neven vanished ahead. He took two steps in and Daniel was alone, staring, uncomprehending, into a darkness so total he could no longer see the condensation on his breath. It was warmer out of the wind but the chill air clung to him, teasing its way under the cuffs of his sleeves and pants legs.

Beneath his clothes, he felt the hairs on his limbs rising. His scalp tightened.

I can't see anything in here. Not even my breath. Not even that. But I am still here. And I am still breathing. Aren't I?

Beyond the wall of black, Neven was moving around. Daniel followed the sounds of his steps, of his boots crushing gravel and scuffing against rough cement.

There was the sound of something heavy being dragged, moved, dropped. Metallic clang. It was obscenely loud in the close space. Each echo and vibration cracked against the walls, sending jolts down his nerves.

Daniel pulled his gloves off with his teeth and jammed them into his back pocket. His bare fingers stung then quickly numbed. He wanted his hands free, an impulse he wasn't sure made much sense. Something instinctive, maybe. Telling him to be ready.

What am I doing here? What's going to happen here?

At the question, his stomach twisted inside of him. Like he wanted to cry. Like he wanted to laugh. Like something inside of him was trying to break free. He choked. "Man, I don't know if I can do this…sober."

"Do something *real* for once in your fucking life," Neven said from his end of the darkness, his voice hard, edged with an old fury. It echoed, raw and harsh and impossibly loud.

For a moment Daniel felt a quiver of unease.

Neven? Not Neven. There's an understanding between us. Neven's just like me. Isn't he?

There was the *tick-tick* of metal on metal and a burst of light chased the shadows to the corners. It dimmed to a steady glow. The lantern was a large camping light. Heavy, by the looks of it. Neven was crouched over it, his face impossibly white in its glare. His profile was stark, pale against black. When he turned to look at Daniel, his eyes were obscured by shadow.

Daniel looked away from him. "Where is she, exactly?" he asked.

Neven got to his feet and stepped away. And Daniel saw the cage. It was set against the far wall, a hulking frame of tight wire, a sheet of tarp rolled up on top of it in a neat coil. It was a large cage, the kind used for transporting animals. Stepping closer and past the light, Daniel saw there was a girl locked inside. She was crouching, her hair hanging in her face, her knees to shoulders, her arms wrapped around her shins. The cage was barely large enough to contain her. The light from the lantern caught her skin and gave it a warm glow, though Daniel knew she had to be freezing, had to be hurting. Naked like that. Confined like that. Her muscles cramping, her spine aching in its rigid curve. He waited for her to exhale, hoping to see a puff of breath. None came.

Ada?

Daniel wished he could see her face.

"You know she's pregnant, right?" Neven asked.

"Yes. I know."

"She asked me to punch her in the stomach. She asked me to punch her as hard as I wanted. She asked me for help. She came to me, you understand? She wanted me to punch her. Hard as I wanted."

"That sounds like her."

Neven frowned in the semi-darkness. His dark eyebrows drawn tight. That unreadable expression. "You don't mind?"

"I don't know if I mind. She was leaving me. Should I?"

"She was leaving you, and she came to me. You know that? I think she loves me." He paused. "I think I love her. But what about you? Do *you* love her?"

Daniel winced at the phrase. He'd never said it to her; she'd never said it to him. This had made sense, before. It wasn't an emotion he understood, and he hadn't thought she understood it much herself. In its own way, wasn't that why he'd thought she was so perfect for him? So right?

"I don't think it ever really worked like that," Daniel said. "Between her and me."

"That's a shame. I thought you two were onto something. You told me 'every great love story involves at least a little blood.' Or something like that. Remember?"

Daniel nodded. "Yes, that's true. I believe it. It's a kind of...love."

"So you *do* love her."

"I don't know. I don't think so. Not now. She wanted to kill my baby. She wanted to leave me. I haven't figured out yet how I feel about that. Not very good, I think."

Neven dropped his hands to his sides. Something that might have been hope drained from his face. He turned to the cage, the movements of his feet louder in the tight space. "What do you want to do with her?" His tone was desolate.

"I told you. I don't know yet. What about you?"

The girl in the cage twitched, shivered. She still hadn't made a sound.

"Me?" Neven paused. "I want to give her everything she ever wanted."

Daniel stepped back. "By all means."

From across the space of dark and light, Daniel saw Neven's lips form a smile.

FIFTY-SIX

What do you do with a woman who can't love? Not herself, not another. Not the life inside her. You teach her to love. You remind her of gratitude. The benefits of closeness. The pure, beauteous ecstasy that exists in reprieve.

He wanted that light in her eyes. That look of something deep within her breaking, that look of surrender, of discovering the joy beneath it. Thick as syrup, rich as blood. Binding.

He touched her fingertips through the bars. Bare skin, cold flesh, her nails split and broken from clawing at the cage, from pulling at the bars. Her hands smeared brown with dried blood. Cuts on her palms and fingers.

"You don't have to do this to yourself," he told her. He told her many times. "I'll come back for you. Every night. You know I will. But you have to give up while I'm gone. You have to realise what I am to you."

He layered the cage with blankets before he pulled the tarp back over it. She wouldn't be warm, but she wouldn't freeze. A compromise between comfort and torment. What his father had done for his mother had been much the same.

And I understand it now, he realised. *I thought I understood it before, but I didn't, not really. How could I have, without the experience myself? I know why he was so sorry, every time. I'm sorry too. Even now. But this is what they mean when they say "cruel to be kind." She's saving me. I'm saving her. It'll be okay. It will.*

He pressed wet sponges against the bars and let her suck them dry. There was beauty in this, the feeding. His father hadn't done that for his mother. Neven wished that he had because this was another level to this beautiful thing, this thing so terrible it could only be powerful. The cage, the care, the silence and the love building just beneath.

When I let her out, it'll be…she'll be…

He tried not to imagine it because his excitement ran too deep and he didn't want it spoiled with fantasy when the time finally arrived.

He spent the nights with her. Wrapped up in his coat, leaning against the wall beside the cage, his wrists resting on his knees. This too was more than his father had done. He rolled back the tarp on the side facing him and peeled back the blankets so that she could see him, and he could just make out the contours of her face, the shadows of her eyes. The stench that came from the cage was unimaginable. Dead skin, sweat, urine. And something metallic and foul, like rotten blood. But he breathed through his mouth and made himself ignore it.

The worse it is now, the better it will be later.

If you love someone, you make sacrifices. You sacrifice yourself. You sacrifice her. And then something better takes its place.

He touched her cold fingers, caught between the bars of the cage. When he felt her tremble, he believed it. Their truth. His and hers.

Ada. You and me.

Her breathing was a little tight, a little low. Sometimes he thought he heard a whistle between rasps, a song coming from somewhere deep in her chest.

He talked to her. He told her all the things about himself he'd thought of saying but hadn't. Had wanted to say before but couldn't. He watched her face to make sure she wasn't sleeping. Her eyes — glassy, stark — stared back.

Sometimes, in moments of silence, Neven thought he heard footsteps. People, moving around outside. Sometimes heavy booted feet squeaking through the snow. Sometimes lighter, slower, a woman moving cautiously through the stillness of late night. Neighbours coming home from business dinners, parties, bars. People walking their dogs. He didn't know. He kept quiet then, and listened. Once or twice he thought the steps were circling the shed. Sometimes he dozed, waiting for them to pass. When he came back to consciousness it was always with a sense of disorientation — his head throbbing; his back aching; his hands numb, twisted between his legs. He woke in cold and confusion — *Where am I? What is this?* — and then he turned and saw the cage beside him. He saw Ada, her eyes open and fixed on him. Staring at him from across her knees. Shivering.

"I want you to tell me your stories," he said. "I've told you mine."

Clutching her fingers through the cage, he leant his head close to hers. And her mouth moved, but he heard no words. Was she trying to talk, or was she mocking him? Her mouth was parched — that was it. He fed her water. The sponge, his fingers, her mouth.

"Tell me, Ada. Tell me again. Try again."

Her eyes, bloodshot even in the semi-darkness, brightened with urgency. Her hands shook. Her lips moved faster. He heard her tongue tapping her palate. Words. Those had to be words. But all he heard was the whistle in her breath, and the wind moving against the walls beyond them.

FIFTY-SEVEN

Daniel found her luggage a week later. Her green hiking backpack crammed with underwear, skirts, dresses, jeans. Her red leather carrycase filled with shoes and books and keepsakes. Two crystal glasses padded with tissue, placed in a cardboard box. Her obsidian necklace, wrapped in a strip of silk, stuffed into the toe of a canvas slingback.

The bags had been left outside his front door sometime while he was at work. There was a note attached to the handle of the carrycase, written in clear print. Not Ada's hand.

Hi Daniel,

Ada left her bags with me, but she hasn't come back for them. Do you know where she is? I guess you can send it all to her, wherever she's gone. I would've called, but don't have your number.

I hope she's okay. Are you okay? Call me?

Jean
137 3346 6614

Jean. Who was Jean? He used to know, but now it escaped him. Was she the bottle blonde or that minxy little redhead? One of Ada's more obscure expat friends, anyway. One of the many she wouldn't entertain the idea of allowing him to fuck.

He crushed the note in his hand and tossed it in the trash. He sat down and stared at the bags, then stood again to retrieve the note and the box of matches they — he! — kept by the stove. He sat down on the couch and burned the note, watching Jean's tight, tidy lettering blacken and twist and dissolve into ash.

Ada. So what's happened to her?

Once or twice in the week he thought he'd seen Neven near his office, walking far ahead of him, his leather jacket too light for the cold, his hands in his pockets, his head bowed. On at least one occasion he thought he'd seen a woman with him, a woman he had almost believed was Ada until he realised her hair was different, a little too long, a little too dark. Something different, anyway. And he'd only seen the backs of their heads.

He hadn't bothered with it. He didn't have the time or inclination to think about her, or about her with him. Or any of that shit. Except now her suitcases had arrived back at their — his! — apartment.

What do you really know about Neven?

The thought came from a cool, remote part of his brain, calm and smooth and clear enough to startle him.

Nothing, he realised. *Or at least, not much. Maybe not much at all.*

The voice returned, and he focused on it, sitting forward with his elbows on his knees. *Ada's still yours, Daniel. You found her first. She married you. How do you feel about some other guy taking her up, just like that? When she's yours. Yours.*

He hadn't thought about what Neven had done with her after he left the shed that night. He'd very deliberately made sure *not* to think about it. The spite in him saying, *I hope he fucks her up*. The part of him that did, in fact, care about her answering. *Let him give her exactly what she wants. If that's what she wants.* These thoughts only, and nothing more.

But what was it that she wanted? And, maybe more importantly, what did Neven want?

Was it possible that she was still out there, trapped in that cage? Neven said she'd asked him to punch her. He hadn't told Daniel if he'd actually done it or not. Or...how hard.

Daniel was sitting very still, very straight. He felt a pulse of something—*panic?*—surge up from his belly and seize his heart. The jolt came fast and was so intense it almost hurt.

"That's my wife," he said to the empty room. To himself.

He found his feet. He grabbed his keys.

* * *

The padlock hung open, hooked through the mesh. Although it wasn't full dark yet, the shed was lost behind an inky haze. For a moment Daniel thought it was just the pollution—and it may have been—but the shed stood too close to Neven's apartment building, and that long, thick shadow fell over it. Ate it whole. The building's outline sharpened as he got closer. The snow on the ground, a little thinner now, had turned hard and grey over the past few days. It cracked under his steps.

Daniel pushed the gate open—it moved in a series of stuttering shrieks—and walked into the narrow concrete space.

The smell that met him was thick, rich, smothering, the stench of sweat and effluent, of open wounds left too long, of spoiled meat and stagnant water. The smell of the city itself, in many ways. Except that was the smell it carried in summer. Not now, not at this time of year when the filth was frozen over, locked under ice. And there was a sick sweetness to it that for a moment made him think of—

No.

"Neven? Are you here?"

He took another step in and nearly tripped over the camper's lantern. His foot crashed against it and it collapsed on its side with a *clang* so loud that Daniel almost screamed, adrenaline sluicing his blood.

Once the echo had stilled, silence returned. He wished he'd brought a torch or a lighter or something—anything—to help him see by.

I'll walk to the back wall. I'll walk slowly, and I'll feel for the cage. Just to find out if it's still there. If the girl—Ada?—is still locked inside of it.

He'd almost reached it when he heard the sob, the sigh, the sound of a voice that had been held in too long, breaking on tears.

"Neven?"

Daniel reached an arm out and his fingers scraped the concrete wall. He stepped closer and his foot bumped against Neven's knee.

"It didn't work," Neven said from below him. "I opened the cage but she wouldn't reach for me. I tried to pull her out, but she wouldn't take my hands. She didn't want to touch me. To hold onto me."

Daniel stood very still for a moment, staring, forcing himself to see. After a minute he made out the shape of the cage. It was just to his left, its hard edges glimmering softly in the black and white fuzz of his weak night vision.

"Is she still inside?"

"Yes."

Daniel thought for a moment. When he spoke, his voice trembled. "Is she…is she breathing?"

"I don't know."

"Goddammit, Neven."

Daniel sank to his haunches and felt along the edges of the cage. The top was open. His hands vanished inside and he felt blindly, groping. He touched something soft, something cold. Something alive? His fingers travelled, trembling. Her thigh? Her shoulder? He moved his hand further back and he felt the feathery taper of her hair. He tugged at it and it came loose in his fingers. Quickly he rose off his knees, bending in, cupping her face. Her mouth was slack – *not rigor mortis, she might not be dead* – her head hung loose on her shoulders.

It was too dark to see her features, to make sure it was her, really her. He ran his fingers along her cheekbones, her chin, trying to recognise the angles. Hoping to read her face the same way a blind man might. This face he'd kissed so many times. This head that she had rested on his chest. Her skin was damp and rubbery, and very cold.

For a moment he remembered her self-portrait. That hideous, mutilated visage.

Dear God is that how she is now? Is that what I'm touching?

His heart twisted in pain, the backs of his eyes burned. "Neven. What did you do? What did you do?"

From behind them came the sound of the gate screaming open. Daniel turned, startled.

There was a woman there, staring in at them. She stood in silhouette, the weak light from outside leaking in behind her. But he knew that shape, that stance—slim shoulders, hair clipped back. Her arms straight at her sides, her shoulders set. Her jacket hung open, the belt buckle was torn at her hip. It swung to the side when she moved. That was her old jacket, the red one, the one that—

"Ada?"

"You sick fuck!" she shrieked at him, at them. Her voice was high and crazed. It cracked along the walls and echoed. For a moment their ears hurt. But that voice, it was hers.

"She's hysterical," Daniel said softly, struck with a mix of gratitude and disbelief. He'd never seen Ada like this before. He'd never seen her in such extreme emotion, not even when she'd told him about the things that had hurt her, scarred her, come closest to breaking her. He'd never heard her raise her voice like this, either. Not in all their years together, not even in the times when he himself had done the most damage to her —

But she's alive!

He wanted to look behind him, to check again and confirm to himself that the thing in the cage was not some shared hallucination, not some crazy psychic meld between him and Neven, centred around some girl, some other girl —

"Neven, she's insane. She's gone crazy." He wasn't sure if he was relieved or horrified.

"No," Neven said. And Daniel didn't see this, but Neven smiled a wide, welcoming smile, his eyes warm with love. "She's not screaming. Or crying. She's *laughing*."

Ada hunched over, her hands on her knees. She glowered in at them, the light catching the side of her face for one brief instant. Painting it monstrous.

"Ada," Daniel said. His heart was beating so fast his whole body shook. *Terrified*, he realised. *I'm terrified. I've never been so afraid. Never been so —*

Neven was stepping past him, moving toward the woman Daniel understood — in a flash-fire of deeper instincts primed now by his panic — was Not Ada, not quite, not really —

A figure stepped in from the side and flanked the Not Ada. A man in a long dark overcoat, his hands in his pockets. *Clenched into fists*, Daniel knew. *He keeps things in his pockets, and he crushes them. Keys, slips of paper, change–anything, anything. He'll crush anything —*

"Daniel?" Neven stopped, glancing back. His eyes were wide, his skin a sick white where the light hit the side of his face. The rest of him in silhouette, too much a part of the shadows for Daniel to see his expression and read what it said.

"Neven, don't—"

The other Daniel removed his hand from his pocket. He stepped into the enclosure, reached toward Neven, and closed his crushing fingers around Neven's throat. There was the crunch-pop of his trachea as it shattered. Neven gurgled a mouthful of blood. Released, he dropped to his knees and fell to his side. He lay there in voiceless agony, froths of blood leaking from his mouth.

There's nothing beautiful about this, Daniel thought from somewhere far outside of himself, watching his friend writhe. *This is hideous. It could only ever be hideous. How did I ever think there was anything good about blood, about pain? What —*

A third man appeared beside Ada.

Female, neuter, male —

This Neven held the gate for the other Daniel to step back through it, and as he did he glanced at the Daniel left behind. He smiled a broad smile. He pulled the gate shut. The padlock clicked home.

"Let me out!"

They stared in at him, watching. Their familiar faces alien and cold.

"What do you want? Let me out!"

Daniel glanced down at Neven on the floor of the shed. He lay with his hands wrapped around his throat, kicking his feet, lost to pain. Daniel snatched a look behind him, as if hoping to see a door or window that had magically appeared.

A way out. Please.

There was only the same damp, foul-smelling darkness. A cage in the shadows, a corpse in the cage. And Daniel left standing alone, locked in an abandoned shed nobody visited and few knew the existence of.

In the city, people forget to listen for the sound of screams.

"Don't do this!" Daniel rushed to the gate toward the three — People? Things? Doubles? — that stood in surreal solidity, stood there staring. Stood there, smiling.

He stopped in front of Ada-not-Ada. So much exactly the same, only her eyes were different, something about them didn't quite strike true. The look in them maybe. So black, so dark.

She reached into her Daniel's front pocket, and she pulled out his small silver blade. Long and smooth and bright, milky-clean.

She slid it through the chain-link, offering it to him.

It was his blade.

It was not his blade.

It shone there for him. Allure in its smooth taper, its vicious point. His goring blade, his slicing blade. The antique blade he'd bought when he was just eighteen and knew that it was his forever.

His fingers closed on the tip. The metal felt hot, searing hot, but familiar, too, and comforting.

He stood there for lost moments, staring down at it, a thing his-not-his, held precious in trembling hands-not-his, telling him to do what he didn't want to do.

When he looked up again, they were gone.

ACKNOWLEGEMENTS

When I first conceived this torture tale, it was with the aim of pushing through as many safe zones as I could handle, sledge-hammering more of my own boundaries than I knew existed. It was an effort in darkest exploration of my own mind, as well as an attempt to capture the essence of what I most admire in extreme horror literature and film. I didn't know what the result would be when I began (all I heard in my own head was *Push!*), and I learned a great deal in the process of tackling some of the themes contained here. That said, no tale is ever truly told alone, and over the year it took me to pen the first draft of *Seeing Double*, I leaned hard on the many inspiring and truly exceptional people I had in my life at that time. So to those specifically mentioned and equally to those not: Your support and encouragement, advice and enlightenment, were essential to the structure I needed in order to write this book.

To the Serbian dudes on *FangJia*. Realer than real, and always laughing. You didn't know you were doing it, but thank you for showing me how things balance even in extremes.

Thanks to Linda Westman, metal drummer and my chaos girl heroine, who cheerfully took the earliest draft of *Seeing Double* home to read... and sweetly never blamed me for the consequences. (Sorry, babe!)

Grazie to Gianluigi Perrone, my horror guru back then, who showed me his incredible film *Morituris*... and taught me that there is a time and a way to be completely unafraid. A lesson I shall keep forever.

Nora: 亲爱的，你真是一个超级棒的女孩儿。我爱你。感谢。

Soul-felt thanks to Edoardo Gagliardi, who was at my side and uncomplaining every day as I went through the process of writing the first draft of this book.

And thanks to Stephanie Christella Rosina Warner, who deserves a very large share of my gratitude regarding this particular work. Thank you for opening my eyes, and thank you for letting me so darkly cast that gaze you offered into my own work. You are a magnificent talent, an incredible being. I'm humbled to call you a friend.

ABOUT THE AUTHOR

Karen Runge is a horror and dark fiction author whose works have appeared in various anthologies and fiction collections from around the world. Her first solo collection, *Seven Sins*, was released in 2016 by Concord Free Press. She currently lives in Johannesburg, South Africa.

MORE DARK FICTION FROM
GREY MATTER PRESS

"Grey Matter Press has managed to establish itself as one of the premiere purveyors of horror fiction currently in existence via both a series of killer anthologies — *SPLATTERLANDS, OMINOUS REALITIES, EQUILIBRIUM OVERTURNED* — and John F.D. Taff's harrowing novella collection *THE END IN ALL BEGINNINGS*."

- FANGORIA Magazine

GREY MATTER
P R E S S

THE **REAL MONSTERS** ARE IN YOUR MIRROR

PEEL BACK THE SKIN

FROM BRAM STOKER AWARD® NOMINATED EDITORS

ANTHONY | SHARON
RIVERA | LAWSON

PEEL BACK THE SKIN
ANTHOLOGY OF HORROR

They are among us.

They live down the street. In the apartment next door. And even in our own homes.

They're the real monsters. And they stare back at us from our bathroom mirrors.

Peel Back the Skin is a powerhouse new anthology of terror that strips away the mask from the real monsters of our time – mankind.

Featuring all-new fiction from a star-studded cast of award-winning authors from the horror, dark fantasy, speculative, transgressive, extreme horror and thriller genres, *Peel Back the Skin* is the next game-changing release from Bram Stoker Award-nominated editors Anthony Rivera and Sharon Lawson.

FEATURING:

Jonathan Maberry	James Lowder
Ray Garton	Lucy Taylor
Tim Lebbon	Joe McKinney
Ed Kurtz	Erik Williams
William Meikle	Charles Austin Muir
Yvonne Navarro	John McCallum Swain
Durand Sheng Welsh	Nancy A. Collins

Graham Masterton

GREY MATTER
P R E S S

greymatterpress.com

DREAD

a head full of bad dreams

JONATHAN MABERRY
BRACKEN MACLEOD
WILLIAM MEIKLE
JOHN C. FOSTER
JOHN F.D. TAFF
MICHAEL LAIMO
TIM WAGGONER
RAY GARTON
JG FAHERTY
JOHN EVERSON
TRENT ZELAZNY
AND MANY MORE

from editors
ANTHONY RIVERA
SHARON LAWSON

THE BEST OF GREY MATTER PRESS VOLUME ONE

DREAD
A HEAD FULL OF BAD DREAMS

There are some nightmares from which you can never wake.

Dread: A Head Full of Bad Dreams is a terrifying volume of the darkest hallucinatory revelations from the minds of some of the most accomplished award-winning authors of our time. Travel dark passageways and experience the alarming visions of twenty masters from the horror, fantasy, science fiction, thriller, transgressive and speculative fiction genres as they bare their souls and fill your head with a lifetime of bad dreams.

Dread is the first-ever reader curated volume of horror from Grey Matter Press. The twenty short stories in this book were chosen solely by fans of dark fiction. *Dread* includes a special Introduction from Bram Stoker Award-nominated editor Anthony Rivera who says:

> "Readers who embrace darkness are souls of conscience with hearts of passion and voices that deserve to be heard. It's from this group of passionate voices that the nightmares in *Dread: A Head Full of Bad Dreams* were born.
> "Turning over the reins of editorial curation for this volume to the readers who matter most may well have been the best decision I've ever made. This book that you've created embodies your passion for dark fiction and serves as your own head of bad dreams come to life."

FEATURING:

Ray Garton	Jonathan Maberry
John F.D. Taff	JG Faherty
William Meikle	John Everson
Rose Blackthorn	Michael Laimo
Bracken MacLeod	John C. Foster
Tim Waggoner	Jane Brooks
Chad McKee	Peter Whitley
T. Fox Dunham	J. Daniel Stone
Edward Morris	Jonathan Balog
Trent Zelazny	Martin Rose

GREY MATTER

P R E S S

greymatterpress.com

MISTER
WHITE

THE NOVEL

DO
NOT
SPEAK
HIS
NAME

JOHN C.
FOSTER

MISTER WHITE
BY JOHN C. FOSTER

In the shadowy world of international espionage and governmental black ops, when a group of American spies go bad and inadvertently unleash an ancient malevolent force that feeds on the fears of mankind, a young family finds themselves in the crosshairs of a frantic supernatural mystery of global proportions with only one man to turn to for their salvation.

Combine the intricate, plot-driven stylings of suspense masters Tom Clancy and Robert Ludlum, add a healthy dose of Clive Barker's dark and brooding occult horror themes, and you get a glimpse into the supernatural world of international espionage that the chilling new horror novel *Mister White* is about to reveal.

John C. Foster's *Mister White* is a terrifying genre-busting suspense shocker that, once and for all, answer the question you dare not ask: "Who is Mister White?"

––––––––––––––

"*Mister White* is a potent and hypnotic brew that blends horror, espionage and mystery. Foster has written the kind of book that keeps the genre fresh and alive and will make fans cheer. Books like this are the reason I love horror fiction." – RAY GARTON, Grand Master of Horror and Bram Stoker Award®-nominated author of *Live Girls* and *Scissors*.

"*Mister White* is like Stephen King's *The Stand* meets Ian Fleming's James Bond with Graham Masterton's *The Manitou* thrown in for good measure. It's frenetically paced, spectacularly gory and eerie as hell. Highly recommended!" – JOHN F.D. TAFF, Bram Stoker Award®-nominated author of *The End in All Beginnings*

––––––––––––––

GREY MATTER
P R E S S

greymatterpress.com

BRAM STOKER AWARD® NOMINATED

THE END
IN ALL
BEGINNINGS

"CHILLING"
- Kealan Patrick Burke

"THE BEST NOVELLA
COLLECTION IN YEARS!"
- Jack Ketchum

JOHN F.D. TAFF
MODERN HORROR'S KING OF PAIN

THE END IN ALL BEGINNINGS
BY JOHN F.D. TAFF

The Bram Stoker Award-nominated *The End in All Beginnings* is a tour de force through the emotional pain and anguish of the human condition. Hailed as one of the best volumes of heartfelt and gut-wrenching horror in recent history, *The End in All Beginnings* is a disturbing trip through the ages exploring the painful tragedies of life, love and loss.

Exploring complex themes that run the gamut from loss of childhood innocence, to the dreadful reality of survival after everything we hold dear is gone, to some of the most profound aspects of human tragedy, author John F.D. Taff takes readers on a skillfully balanced emotional journey through everyday terrors that are uncomfortably real over the course of the human lifetime. Taff's highly nuanced writing style is at times darkly comedic, often deeply poetic and always devastatingly accurate in the most terrifying of ways.

Evoking the literary styles of horror legends Mary Shelley, Edgar Allen Poe and Bram Stoker, *The End in All Beginnings* pays homage to modern masters Stephen King, Ramsey Campbell, Ray Bradbury and Clive Barker.

"*The End in All Beginnings* is accomplished stuff, complex and heartfelt. It's one of the best novella collections I've read in years!" – JACK KETCHUM, Bram Stoker Award®-winning author of *The Box, Closing Time* and *Peaceable Kingdom*

"Taff brings the pain in five damaged and disturbing tales of love gone horribly wrong. This collection is like a knife in the heart. Highly recommended!" – JONATHAN MABERRY, *New York Times* bestselling author of *Code Zero* and *Fall of Night*

GREY MATTER
P R E S S

greymatterpress.com

COMING SOON
FROM GREY MATTER PRESS

Before by Paul Kane

Little Black Spots by John F.D. Taff

Little Deaths: 5th Anniversary Edition by John F.D. Taff

The Madness of Crowds: The Ladies Bristol Occult Adventures #2 by Rhoads Brazos

MORE TITLES
FROM GREY MATTER PRESS

The Devil's Trill: The Ladies Bristol Occult Adventures #1 by Rhoads Brazos

Dark Visions: A Collection of Modern Horror - Volume One

Dark Visions: A Collection of Modern Horror - Volume Two

Death's Realm: The Anthology

Dread: The Best of Grey Matter Press - Volume One

The End in All Beginnings by John F.D. Taff

Equilibrium Overturned: A Volume of Apocalyptic Horrors

I Can Taste the Blood

Mister White: The Novel by John C. Foster

The Night Marchers and Other Strange Tales by Daniel Braum

Ominous Realities

Peel Back the Skin: Anthology of Horror

Savage Beasts

Secrets of the Weird by Chad Stroup

Seeing Double by Karen Runge

Splatterlands

RETURNING IN 2017
FROM GREY MATTER PRESS

The Bell Witch by John F.D. Taff

Kill/ Off by John F.D. Taff

SEEING DOUBLE

KAREN RUNGE

25742508R10156

Printed in Great Britain
by Amazon